A DOG'S PURPOSE

Ellie's Story

W. BRUCE CAMERON is *The New York Times* bestselling author of *A Dog's Purpose*, now a major motion picture, *A Dog's Journey* and *A Dog for Christmas*. *A Dog's Purpose: Ellie's Story* was his first book for young readers. He lives in California.

Also by
W. Bruce Cameron

A Dog's Purpose: Bailey's Story

A Dog's Purpose

A Dog's Journey

A Dog for Christmas

A DOG'S PURPOSE

Ellie's Story

W. Bruce Cameron

MACMILLAN CHILDREN'S BOOKS

First published in the US 2015 by Tom Doherty Associates, LLC

First published in the UK 2017 by Macmillan Children's Books
an imprint of Pan Macmillan
20 New Wharf Road, London N1 9RR
Associated companies throughout the world
www.panmacmillan.com

ISBN 978-1-5098-5364-9

For Eloise and Gordon

1

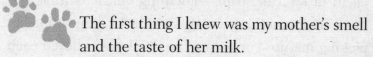The first thing I knew was my mother's smell and the taste of her milk.

I had to fight my way to her, struggling over and around the soft, fuzzy bodies of my brothers and sisters, to reach that milk and fill my empty stomach. I squirmed and pushed with my feeble legs, inching forward, until I could taste the warm sweetness spilling over my tongue.

In a few days my eyes were open and I could see my mother's dark brown face and the pale blue blanket that she lay on, though at first everything was very blurry.

Sometimes, when I felt lonely or cold or lost, I'd whimper, pressing closer to her. My brother and sisters always got confused and took my whimpers for signs of weakness. Then they'd jump on me. There were seven

1

of them, all brown with black markings, and I couldn't understand why it was so hard for them to figure out who was going to be in charge around here.

When it wasn't Mother, it was going to be me. I was, in my opinion, the smartest puppy.

A woman with soft hands and a softer voice often came down a set of stairs to see us. On the first day my mother growled at her, just a little, and the woman was careful to stay back. But later my mother seemed to change her mind and decided that it was all right for the woman to pick us up, cuddle us, and hold us close.

She had an interesting smell, this woman. Something clean (a kind of soap), something delicious (that was food), and something that was just her. I didn't mind her picking me up – or not much. But I was relieved each time she laid me gently back down on the blanket beside my mother.

A man sometimes came down the stairs to look at us, too, and to bring a dish of food and a bowl of water for my mother. That water! The first time I went near the bowl to sniff at it, one of my brothers knocked into me from behind and I fell face-first into the bowl.

Cold! Water went up my nose and stung my eyes, and when I tried to whimper and let my mother know that I needed help water rushed into my mouth, too. It took all my strength to heave myself up out of that slippery bowl and shake my fur clean and dry. After that I stayed away from the water bowl as much as I could. My brother acted as if nothing happened, though it was clearly all his fault.

After a few weeks, when my legs were stronger, the man came down the stairs holding something big and brown. He set the brown thing down on the floor and gently picked up one of my brothers, popping him inside.

'In the box, buddy,' the man said. 'Don't worry. It won't be for long.'

My brother yelped. I could hear him, but I couldn't see him! All of us started yipping and barking as the man picked us up, one by one, and put us where he had put my brother – in the box.

It was like being in a tiny room, with a floor and walls of something smooth and slippery. My tiny claws slipped and slid. They slipped and slid even worse when the man lifted the box into the air.

My brothers and sisters scrambled all over each other, trying to figure out what was happening. I stood on two sisters and hooked my paws over the edge of the box and peeked out. The man was climbing up the stairs, and my mother was trotting behind him. That made me feel better. We could not be going anywhere dangerous if Mother was coming.

'Whoops, back inside, girl,' said the man. 'Don't fall out.'

He gently pushed my paws off the box's edge, and I landed on the same idiot brother who had knocked me into the water bowl. He chewed on my foot before I yanked it away.

The man carried us for a little while longer and then set the box down. One by one he and the woman lifted us out.

We were somewhere incredible. It was called Outside.

The light was the first thing. It was so bright I could barely see for several minutes. Then there was something strange under my paws – something springy and soft, like the blanket, but prickly. Grass! I bit it, to show it who was boss. It didn't bite back, so I figured that was settled. I was in charge of the grass.

And the smells! I had learned the smells of my mother and my littermates and the blanket where we had lived and of the woman and the man who came to visit us. But now the air was moving, blowing past me and tickling my nose with a million smells that I couldn't sort out. My brothers and sisters rushed past me, yelping, stumbling, falling on their faces, and rolling on to their sides. I stood still, with my nose in the air, trying to understand where I was.

The grass underfoot smelt sharp and fresh. There was another smell underneath that, dark and dense and rich. It smelt like something that would be good to dig.

The moving air brought more smells from further away – something smoky and tasty from inside the house, something sweet from the bushes alongside it, something harsh and sour and stinking that roared by, too fast, on the other side of a tall wooden fence.

And something mysterious and furry and alive, like me.

That smell was a grown-up dog in a pen. My mother trotted over to him, and they touched noses through a wire fence. I knew this other dog was male, like my brothers, and I sensed that he was important to Mother. Without knowing how, I knew this dog was my father.

'He seems like he'll be fine with the puppies,' the man said to the woman.

'You going to be OK, Bernie? You want to come out?' Our father's name was Bernie. The woman opened his cage. He bounded out, sniffed at us, and then went over to pee on the fence.

We all galloped after him, falling over every minute but getting up again. Bernie put his face down and one of my brothers jumped up and bit at Bernie's ears. Very disrespectful! But he didn't seem to mind. He just shook his head, sending my brother rolling over.

Some of the other pups took that for an invitation and pounced on Bernie. He knocked a few of them gently aside, sniffed at the rest, and came over to me.

I didn't bite at him or jump on him, so I got to stay

on my feet. But he put his nose down and sniffed me all over, then put a paw on top of me, just because.

I knew I should not fight back. I might have been in charge of my littermates, even if some of them had strange ideas about that. But this father dog, like Mother, was in charge of me. I let him squash me down into the soft, springy grass and hold me there for a few seconds before Bernie wandered off to let the man pet him and scratch behind his ears.

After that we did Outside every day. I learned that the dark, fascinating stuff under the grass was dirt. And I also learned how to make sure my brothers and sisters didn't get the wrong idea about me. They would creep up behind me and pounce or race across the yard to barrel into me, so I would have to snarl and show my teeth or roll over and over until I was on top. Then I'd walk away and later take the chance to sneak up on them.

It was funny how they didn't just accept that I was the boss. They'd wrestle and wriggle and try to squash me down with their tiny paws, the way Bernie had done with his big one. They were not Father or Mother, though, so I never let them get away with it. But they kept trying.

Bernie sometimes played with us a little, too, and the woman came out with funny-smelling things for us to chew on. 'Here are your toys, pups,' she'd say.

Then one day a new man came into the yard. He had different ideas about playing. First he clapped his hands loudly. One of my brothers yelped and ran to Mother. Several more of the puppies jumped back a few steps, and one whimpered. I was startled, too, but something told me there was no danger. The man picked up the ones who hadn't seemed scared and put us in a box, carrying us away to a different section of the yard.

One by one, he lifted us out. When it was my turn, he put me down on the grass and then he turned and walked away from me, as if he'd forgotten I was even there. I followed him, curious to see what he'd do next.

'Good dog!' he told me. A good dog, just for following him? This guy was a pushover.

Then the man took something out of his pocket. He opened it up and put the soft folds over me. 'Hey, girl, can you find your way out of the T-shirt?' he asked.

I had no idea what was going on, but I didn't like it. The white cotton was all over the place, as if I were wrapped up in a blanket. I tried to fight it, showing it who was boss, just as I did with my littermates. That didn't work. I could scratch it or bite it, but it didn't go away. It just clung to me, all over my face, all over my body.

I tried to walk, figuring maybe I would get away from it. The T-shirt walked with me. I growled and shook my head hard. That helped a little. The cloth fell away from my face, and I got a glimpse of green grass near my tail.

My tail! That was it! The way to get out of this thing was to back up. I did that, shaking my head again to shuffle the shirt off me. In a few seconds I was out on the grass. The man was nearby, so I ran over to him for more praise.

The woman had come out into the yard to watch.

'Most of them take a minute or two to puzzle it out, but this one's pretty bright,' the man remarked. He knelt down and took hold of me, flipping me over on to my back in the grass. I squirmed. It wasn't fair. He was so much bigger than I was!

'She doesn't like that, Jakob,' the woman said.

'None of them like it. The question is, will she stop struggling and let me be the boss or will she keep fighting? I got to have a dog that knows I'm the boss,' the man replied to the woman.

I heard the word 'dog', and it didn't sound angry. I wasn't being punished. But I *was* being pinned down. It was kind of like the way Bernie had pushed me down into the grass, the first day I had met him. And this man *was* bigger than me, the way Bernie was bigger. Maybe that meant this man was supposed to be in charge, the way Father was.

Anyway, I figured I didn't know what kind of game we were playing now, so I just relaxed. No more struggling.

'Good dog!' the man said again. I guessed his name

was Jakob. He sure had some strange ideas on how to play with a puppy.

Next he took something flat and white from his pocket and crumpled it up. It made the most fascinating noise while he was doing that! I wished I could get a better look – and more than that, I wished I could get a taste. What *was* this new thing?

'Want it, girl? Want the paper?' Jakob said.

I wanted it! He moved it around in front of my face, and I chased it, snapping, trying to get a hold on it. I couldn't do it! My mouth was too small, and my head moved too slowly. Then the man flipped the thing into the air and I raced after it. Pounce! I landed on it with both my front paws and settled down to chew it. *Ha! Try to get it now!*

It tasted interesting but not as good as I thought it would. It had been more fun when it was moving anyway. I picked it up and brought it back to the man, dropping it at his feet. Then I plopped my rear end into the grass and wagged my tail, hoping he'd get the hint and throw it again.

'This one,' Jakob said. 'I'll take this one.'

2

Jakob scooped me up and carried me out of the yard. I was amazed. Outside was bigger than I had ever thought. It went on forever!

In front of the house, big, loud things zoomed past, smelling of metal and smoke and other sharp and unpleasant odours. I had no idea what these things were, but I was pretty sure they were dangerous. Jakob opened the back of one, and I squirmed against his chest and whimpered.

'It's OK, girl,' Jakob said. 'Just a quick ride in the truck. Don't worry about it. OK? Just a truck.'

Truck. His tones were soothing, but I was plenty worried. I didn't want to go anywhere in anything that smelt like this.

There was something like a box, only made out of metal, in the back of the truck. Jakob opened it up with one hand and with the other dumped me gently inside.

Then he left me. He left me!

This was *not* right. I was sure about it. Of course I didn't like the idea of being taken away from my mother and brothers and sisters, but something told me that it was the way things had to be. Dogs were supposed to be with people. Jakob was going to be my family now.

But that meant Jakob was supposed to be *with* me! He wasn't supposed to go far away and leave me in a cold metal box in the back of a loud, smelly truck!

I barked. I whimpered. I did everything I could to let Jakob know he had made a mistake and was supposed to come back. But he must not have heard me, because he didn't show up to take me out of the box. I heard a loud *thump* and then the metal box started to shake, and we were *moving*. It was just like being carried in a box out into the yard, my body rocking back and forth. I really didn't like this! The truck growled and roared and I was pretty sure it was going to eat me. Where was Jakob?

My frantic barking must have got through to him at last, because he came back and took me out of the cage when the truck finally stopped moving. 'Not too bad, huh, girl?' he said to me.

He seemed awfully cheerful after what we'd just

been through together. Still, I was so grateful that he had returned I didn't hold a grudge. I just rested against his chest as he carried me up several flights of stairs and into my new home.

There was a lot to explore. A kitchen, with fascinating smells and little doors that I couldn't open, even when I pawed at them. A living room, with a couch that smelt like Jakob and a box that made noise sometimes. A balcony, where I could sit with Jakob and look over houses and yards and trees and more zooming, loud things like the truck.

There was a bedroom, with a big bed that smelt like Jakob, too. I tried to climb up on it the first day, and Jakob firmly dumped me off. 'No, girl. *This* is your bed,' he said, and showed me a soft, furry circle on the floor. It felt a little like the blanket I used to sleep on with Mother and my littermates, but it didn't smell like them. It smelt empty and cold.

What I liked the best, though, was the park. Jakob took me there more than once that first day. There was more of the springy grass that was fun to run around on, and Jakob tossed some sticks for me to pounce on and bring back. Then he pulled a little round thing from his pocket and threw it for me. I chased it down and tried to get my tiny mouth around it.

Then a little animal darted past, shaking a strangely fuzzy tail. I dropped the ball immediately and dashed after it. This was much more fun!

Obviously the animal was made for chasing. It zigged and zagged across the grass and headed for a tree. To my astonishment, it went straight up the trunk! I tried it myself and fell over on my back. The animal sat on a high branch and laughed at me as I ran around the trunk yapping in frustration. Why wouldn't my paws take me up? The little animal had done it so easily!

Jakob came to sit beside me and scratch behind my ears. 'Don't give up, girl,' he told me. 'Never give up. Now, I can't keep calling you girl. Elleya.' I wondered what he was talking about. 'It's Swedish for "moose". You're a Swedish shepherd, now.' I knew he was talking to me, so I wagged, even though his words made no real sense. 'Elleya, Elleya,' he said, and moved a little away from me. 'Come, Ellie, Come.'

Pretty soon I started to recognize that word, 'Come'. It was one of Jakob's favourites. When he said it, I'd sometimes wander over to see what was going on and he'd pet me and give me something tasty from his hand. 'Come' meant praise and petting and a treat, so pretty soon I always showed up for it. But my favourite words from him were 'Good dog!' 'Good dog!' always meant he would pet me, rubbing my fur until I wriggled from my toes to my tail with happiness. His hands smelt of oil and his truck and of papers and other people.

Jakob never seemed to get angry about anything,

even when my little bladder signalled that it was full and let go all in one rush. When I did manage to get outside before anything happened, he gave me such praise that I decided I'd try to do it as much as possible, since it seemed to please him so much.

I wanted to make Jakob happy. I just wasn't sure how.

He was patient with me, always. He petted me and called me Good Dog and seemed to like having me nearby. But I could tell that he wasn't happy. When he wasn't taking me out for walks, he mostly sat on the couch. Sometimes he'd turn on the talking box; sometimes he just sat or lay down flat and looked at the ceiling. If I went over and nuzzled at his hand, he'd rub my ears a little, but never for long.

I would sigh and lie down beside him. I thought he'd probably feel better if he let me up on the couch with him, and so would I – but I'd learned that wasn't going to happen.

On our first night together, Jakob had watched the noisy box for a while and then he'd yawned and wandered into the bedroom. I followed him. After he'd undressed, he crawled under the covers on the bed. It looked so comfortable that I immediately went up after him. It was all I could do to leap so high, so I figured I was due for some praising and maybe a treat.

Instead, he got out of bed and put me back into the

furry circle on the floor. 'This is your bed,' he told me. 'Yours, Ellie.'

He climbed back into the big bed. I could see he didn't want me to join him up there, but I couldn't understand why. He had so much room! My bed was comfortable, but it was lonely. I was used to sleeping with Mother and my brothers and sisters. This was not at all the same. I whimpered, to let Jakob know something was wrong.

'You'll get used to it, Ellie,' I heard him say from the big bed. 'We all have to get used to being alone.'

After some time I got used to it, but that didn't mean I liked it. I still tried to sneak under Jakob's covers every now and then. He never shouted or pushed me, but he never let me stay. In a few minutes I'd be back in my own bed. After a while I decided it was less trouble just to stay there.

For a few days, Jakob was home with me all the time. Then one morning, he got dressed in different clothes. Everything he wore was a dark colour, and he pulled on a heavy belt with things hanging from it. 'Got to go to work, Ellie girl,' he told me. 'Don't worry, I'll be home soon.'

Then he left.

This did not seem right. I hadn't liked it when Jakob had left me alone in the truck, but he had come back. I remembered that. He'd come back this time, too. I settled in to wait.

Waiting was very hard.

I lay in my bed for a while, but then I nosed my way under Jakob's blankets. They smelt like him, and that was comforting. But after a while I got restless and went to the living room so I could look out of the glass door that led to the balcony. Maybe I'd see Jakob from there.

I didn't.

I sniffed the couch cushions. They smelt like Jakob. I chewed a little on one of the rubber bones he'd got me. It was odd to chew something with so little taste, but my teeth *wanted* to gnaw something and Jakob said, 'Good dog!' when I bit this. So I chewed it and waited some more.

Jakob still hadn't come back.

Maybe this time he'd really forgotten me. Or maybe something had happened to him! Maybe he was hurt and couldn't come back to get me! Maybe he needed me! How could I get to him, shut up in this? I paced back and forth in front of the door, whining.

Then the lock made a clicking noise. I jumped back. The door swung open. Jakob! He'd come back!

'Oh, hello there, sweetie!' cooed a voice.

It wasn't Jakob at all.

It was a woman. She came in as if she belonged here, and sat right down on the floor, putting out her hands to me.

'There, there, sweetie, don't worry. I'm Georgia. I'm here to take you out. Oh, aren't you cute. Aren't you the cutest thing! You're Ellie, right? You're Ellie-wellie Cuddle-Coo. Come here, Ellie, sweetie; come to Georgia.'

I knew that word, 'Come'. Was this woman like Jakob? Did she want me to move closer to her? I did it, and she petted and praised me. 'Good girl, Ellie. Good girl!' She clipped the leash on to my collar and took me outside to the park.

I decided I liked Georgia very much.

She laughed when I chased the small, fuzzy animals, and she petted me a lot, rubbing her hands through my fur, talking to me in a stream of words. None of it made any sense, except for 'Ellie' and 'Come', but I liked hearing her anyway. She was happy to see me. She was happy to be with me. She was happy in a way Jakob never was.

But then Georgia left, too. She brought me back to the apartment, petted me, checked that I had water in my bowl, kissed me between my ears (Jakob definitely never did that!), and went out the door.

These people! Why didn't they understand that a dog was supposed to be *with* humans? Not left behind in an apartment. Not chewing on a tasteless rubber bone. I tried to sleep, tried to chew my bone, but mostly paced around, whining a little in frustration, until the

17

door creaked again and Georgia came back to take me out once more. Finally, when I thought I couldn't stand it any longer, Jakob came home.

I ran to him and got so excited I jumped up on my back legs. 'Off!' he said sternly, and pushed me back to the floor. Of all the words I'd heard so far, 'Off' was my least favourite. But then he petted me and rubbed my ears, sighed at a puddle on the floor, took me outside to the park, and brought me back to feed me dinner. After that he went to sleep in the big bed while I curled up alone in my little one.

That was the way things went until we started Work.

'Let's go to work,' Jakob said one day. I was a bit older, then, and Georgia had started coming only once a day to walk me while Jakob was gone. Jakob seemed as calm as ever, but I could tell there was something extra under the calmness, some kind of excitement. Work must be something important.

At first Work was just more words. I was already pretty good at Come. Now Jakob took me to the park and taught me Drop, which meant to lie down, and Stay. That was a hard one. I would Drop and then Jakob would walk away from me, as if he'd forgotten (again!) that it was my job to be near him. But I had to stay, with my belly in the grass, until I heard 'Come!' Then I bounded after him. It took me a little while, but I got good at Stay. I could tell that Jakob was pleased, and I was glad.

Jakob didn't love me the way Georgia did. It didn't make him happy just to see me. But it did make him happy when we did Work together. So I decided there and then to be very, very good at Work.

If it made Jakob even a little bit happy, it was what I should be doing. But I still loved the times Georgia would come to see me and call me Ellie-wellie Cuddle-Coo.

After I'd got good at my words, Work changed. Jakob took me to a new place. There were lots of trees and plenty of those distracting little animals – I knew now that they were called squirrels. But I did my best to stay near Jakob, waiting patiently until he showed me what kind of Work he wanted me to do.

A man got out of a car a little way away and walked over to us, waving. 'Hey there, Jakob!' he called out cheerfully.

'Wally,' Jakob said, nodding.

'This the new dog?'

'This is Ellie.'

Wally bent down to pet me. 'You're a big girl, Ellie, huh? You going to be good at this?'

'I think she will,' Jakob said quietly. 'Let's see.'

Wally did something odd then. He ran away.

'What's he doing, Ellie? Where's he going?' Jakob asked.

I watched Wally, who was looking over his shoulder at me.

'Find him! Find!' Jakob told me.

I could tell from his voice that this was a new word he wanted me to learn. But I wasn't sure what I should do. Something to do with Wally. There was Wally, over there, waving excitedly. I started towards him. Was this right? Was it what Jakob wanted me to do?

Wally saw me coming and dropped down to his hands and knees, clapping and smiling. When I caught up to him he showed me a stick. I loved sticks! I grabbed it right away, and Wally hung on so that we could have an excellent game of tug. This was fun! Much better than Drop and Stay.

Then Wally got up, brushing off his knees. 'Look, Ellie. What's he doing? Find him!' Wally said.

I looked around. Didn't 'Find' mean I should go to Wally? But I was right next to Wally! What was I supposed to do?

Jakob was strolling off, so I ran after him. I'd always rather be near Jakob anyway. 'Good dog!' Jakob told me, and played with a stick, too. My tail thrashed with happiness.

Honestly, I thought the game of Find was a little dull. But Wally and Jakob seemed to like it, so we played more of it that afternoon. I was willing to do it for Jakob, especially if it meant I got to play tug-on-a-stick. That, to me, beat Find Wally hands down.

I was doing Work and doing it right. Jakob had called me a good dog. This game of Find was important to him, so I would try my best to learn it. I wanted to be a good dog for Jakob. I even dreamed about Finding Wally. They were happy dreams.

Sometimes, though, I would dream a bad dream about a boy named Ethan. In the dream, Ethan was swimming in cool green water and then suddenly he would slip beneath the surface. Fear would grip me as I watched him go down until with a cry I would lower my head and plunge after him, eyes and mouth open, straining to reach the boy, who kept sinking, sinking, sinking, just out of reach.

When I awoke from this dream I was often panting and would wander the house sniffing. The dream felt real, meaning it felt as if it had really happened.

Why did I keep having that dream?

3

Jakob took me back to the park nearly every day, and Wally was always there. Sometimes a friend of Wally's, Belinda, would come, too.

The game of Find got harder and harder to play. Wally would run faster, or start further away, or duck behind a tree or a bush. He couldn't fool me, though. I always would Find him. And that always meant praise and petting and a good wrestle with a stick. The stick still was the best part, as far as I was concerned.

One day the rules changed. Find Wally got harder than ever.

Jakob and I were at the park, but Wally was not there. Fine. Maybe Jakob would throw a stick for me. He didn't usually do that during Work, but when he was just taking me for a walk in the evenings a stick was often involved, or the ball he carried in his pocket.

But he didn't do that, this time. Instead he looked at me and said, 'Find!'

Huh? Find what? Wally wasn't there.

Where *was* Wally, anyway?

I began to sniff at the ground. I would know a Wally smell if my nose came across it. His sweat, his skin, the soap he used, and a sharp-smelling gum that he liked to chew – all of those things were mixed into the smell that was Wally. Was he around here somewhere? I'd like to know. He might have a stick, since Jakob didn't seem inclined to throw one.

'Good girl, Ellie. Good dog. Find!'

Was I being a good dog? Jakob had called me a good dog just for sniffing? I sniffed harder and walked a few steps. And there it was! The smell that meant Wally! It was strong and fresh. He'd been here not long ago.

What was he doing, running away before I could Find him? Didn't he know this wasn't the way the game was supposed to be played?

I followed the trail that Wally had made. Jakob followed me. He didn't tell me I was a good dog again; he was silent, as if he didn't want to distract me. But I could tell he was pleased. I must be doing this right.

There was a delicious smell close by the trail. It smelt like a sandwich Jakob ate sometimes – bread, roast beef, a strange, spicy sauce (how could humans like that stuff?), and some odd plant things that Jakob sometimes ate, too. I glanced up. A sandwich wrapper was lying in the grass. It smelt so good, my mouth began to water.

'Find, Ellie. Find!' Jakob insisted.

I pulled my nose away from the wrapper. This was Work. I could not let myself be distracted. The rules had changed, but the game was still the same. I was supposed to Find Wally.

So I didn't stop trying, even when the trail got difficult. It ran around a bench, and two people sitting there smiled at me. One of them, a woman, offered me her hand. I smelt something in it, something delectable – a bite of bagel smeared with cream cheese. Yum! Sometimes Jakob dropped a piece of his breakfast bagel in my bowl. I loved it. I'd love this, too. I took a step towards the bench.

'Please don't,' Jakob said behind me. 'She's working.'

'Oh, sorry,' the woman answered, pulling her hand back.

But I already had my nose back to the ground. Bagels and cream cheese were very nice, but they weren't what the game of Find was about. When another dog, a silly, long-legged puppy with a frantically lashing tail, bounced up to me, putting both front legs flat on the ground and asking to play, I ignored him. This was not play. This was Work. Jakob and I did Work together. We had no time for puppy games.

Finally, the trail led me beneath some trees. I smelt several dogs who'd been there before me. Three or four had peed on a big clump of grass. I was tempted to squat and add my own contribution, just so they'd know I'd been here, too, and that they didn't have these woods to themselves.

But Wally was around here somewhere. The trail was stronger and stronger now, and I was getting excited. My tail started to wag. My ears were forward, straining. My nose had never been so busy before. Wally? Wally? I was almost on top of him . . .

And then I was. The trail led me around a tree with a wide trunk, and on the other side was Wally, stretched out on the grass and leaning back on a thick root.

The minute he saw me, he jumped up. 'You did it, Ellie! You Found me!'

'Good girl. Good dog!' Jakob praised.

There was the stick and I enjoyed it, but even more I enjoyed the tone of Jakob's voice. 'She's good, huh? I was hardly here ten minutes!' Wally said to Jakob.

'She's good,' Jakob agreed quietly.

'She could really be something special.'

Jakob rubbed behind my ears. 'I think she could.'

After that Wally was never there when we got to the park, and I always had to Find him wherever he had wandered off to. Jakob stopped following me, and I learned two new words: 'Show me!' This meant taking Jakob to where I'd found Wally sprawled under a tree or sitting behind a bush. Or sometimes it even meant showing Jakob where I'd found one of Wally's socks or a T-shirt lying on the ground. (The man was a disaster, always leaving his clothes around for us to Find and pick up.) Somehow, Jakob always knew when I'd Found something after I came running back to him. 'Show me!' he'd say, but only if I had something to show.

I was starting to feel pretty good about Work when Jakob took me to a new place. It was like a park with a playground in it. I knew about playgrounds; there was one at the park where we went in the evenings. Young humans would run around it like puppies, climbing up ladders, barrelling down slides, swooping high into the sky on swings. They certainly looked like they were having fun. But there weren't any children at this playground, and I didn't know how I was supposed to Find Wally here, where there were no trees or bushes for him to hide behind.

First Jakob took me up to a plank that was tipped over, with one end resting on the ground and the other high in the air. I sniffed, but Wally wasn't nearby. I couldn't pick up his scent at all.

It turned out there was more to Work than Find Wally. Jakob tugged gently on my leash, showing me he wanted me to walk up the ramp. Fine. I walked up it. On the other side was a ladder going down.

This side I didn't like as much. Where were my feet supposed to go? I put one paw hesitantly on a rung. Then the next.

'Good dog, Ellie. Keep going,' Jakob encouraged me.

I was eager to be on the nice, safe ground again, so I leaped to the ground.

'No, don't jump,' Jakob said.

I didn't know what he was saying, but the word 'no' I certainly recognized. It was one of my least favourite words.

Jakob took me up the ramp and down the ladder again and again, and after a while I got it: he wanted me to take a step at a time, even though it wasn't the fastest way to the ground. 'Good dog, Ellie!' I loved being a good dog.

The next thing to try was a stack of logs. They were uneven under my feet, and that was a little disturbing. I was used to grass or dirt or pavements, or to smooth floors and carpets indoors. I had to balance and leap from one log to the next.

'Come, Ellie. Good dog, Ellie!'

Jakob's voice encouraged me, and I kept going.

Then came the tube.

Jakob showed it to me, and I sniffed it carefully. Still no sign of Wally, though I supposed he could have squeezed in there with a little effort. I could smell a hint of dogs who'd been here before me. Other than that, it just smelt of plastic.

Jakob went to the other side of the tube. 'Come, Ellie. Come!' he called.

Come through *the tube?*

I knew I was supposed to obey right away. There was never any fooling around during Work. No hesitation. Work meant to do what Jakob said and to do it quickly.

But that tube was dark. Where exactly would it take me?

'Come!'

One more word from Jakob was all that it took. I plunged into the tube, nose first. My front paws clawed at the smooth plastic. My back feet shoved. It was cramped and hot, and the plastic smelt strange. I didn't like the feeling. The walls of the tube were all around me, pressing in on me. I wanted to get through, to get out, to get where Jakob and his voice were waiting for me.

One last wriggle, one frantic shove with my back paws, and I was tumbling on to the fresh-smelling grass.

'Good, Ellie. Good dog!' Jakob's hands were in my fur, petting and scratching, and I was panting a little. It hadn't been easy, but I had done my Work.

We went back to that playground-park many times, and I got quick at all the climbing and balancing and crawling Jakob asked of me. I never grew to like the tube, but I didn't let Jakob know. I'd dive in as soon as I heard his command and wiggle through as quickly as I possibly could.

Jakob showed me a harness, too, a floppy orange thing that looked like a shirt. The first time he put it on me, I wondered if he wanted me to find a way to wriggle out of it, as I'd done with that T-shirt so long ago. But it turned out that wasn't the idea.

'OK, Ellie, hold still while I put your harness on,' Jakob said, and he clipped something on to my back. Then he stepped away.

I looked at him, confused. What was about to happen?

Something pulled on my back. I twitched with surprise and tried to twist my head around. But I couldn't see. The pull got stronger and stronger, and I was lifted right off my feet!

'Ellie, it's OK. Ellie, it's fine. You're all right,' Jakob said firmly. 'Sometimes a rescue dog needs to be hoisted.'

I was not at all sure about any of this. My paws were off the ground! I wanted to run away, but how could I do that when all I could touch was air? I didn't panic, though. Jakob's voice was steady and reassuring. He was watching me with that look he only had when we were Working. So this must be part of Work, and that meant I should accept it, no matter how strange it might feel.

In a minute or two, I had been hauled up to a platform a few feet above the ground. Jakob quickly climbed up beside me and unclipped the cable from my harness. 'Good girl, Ellie. Good dog! You're brave, aren't you, girl?' I was still shaking a little, and he ran his hands through my fur until I felt calm. We practised the harness on other days, and I learned that it never took long before I was back on my feet.

Another time Jakob took something out of a special pocket at his side. He showed it to me.

'Good girl, Ellie. This is a gun. See?'

I saw it and I sniffed at it, but I was glad when he didn't throw it for me to fetch. It didn't look like it would fly far, and it smelt odd. I didn't think I wanted it in my mouth.

Jakob pointed the thing in the air and it made a horrible bang that hurt my ears. I jumped and whined. But when he did it a few more times, I decided that it was simply noise. I didn't like it, but it wasn't going to hurt me.

'No reason to be afraid,' Jakob promised. 'It's a gun, Ellie. A gun. It makes a loud noise, but you're not afraid, are you, girl?'

I wasn't afraid. Guns, it seemed, were part of Work. And Work was nothing to be scared of.

4

A few days after Jakob had shown me the gun, he took me to a new park. There were several people – most of them men, a few women – sitting at long tables, and I noticed that a lot of them had guns as well. They called out to us.

'Sit down, Jakob!'

'This the new dog?'

'Haven't seen you in a while!'

'Hey, Jakob made it! Somebody take a picture!'

This didn't seem to be Work. The people at the table were talking and laughing and eating. I found a crisp on the ground – delicious! – and went to lie down near Jakob, hoping for more.

Jakob was eating and someone had given him a

brown bottle to drink from, but he wasn't talking or laughing, like the rest of them.

'Isn't that right, Jakob?' someone said.

Jakob didn't answer. I sat up and nuzzled his hand. He petted me, but I could sense he wasn't really thinking about me.

'I said, "Isn't that right, Jakob?"'

Jakob turned and looked at everyone watching him, and I sensed his embarrassment. 'What?'

'If there's ever a riot in the city, we're going to need every K-9 unit we can get.'

'Ellie's not that kind of dog,' Jakob said coldly, not looking at anyone in particular. 'She doesn't attack people.'

I straightened up at the sound of my name, in case this was Work after all and a command was coming next. It didn't. But everyone was looking at me now. I moved a little closer to Jakob. When the rest of them started talking again, it was to each other. No one spoke to Jakob. I nuzzled his hand again, and this time he scratched my ears.

'Good dog, Ellie,' he said softly. 'Let's go for a walk, huh?'

Walk? That was a word I knew, and one I liked. I wagged my tail with enthusiasm. A walk was almost as good as more crisps.

There was another playground at this park, the

human kind, and some paths that wound around. I barked at one squirrel that was enough of a show-off to run past a foot away, but mostly I just walked at Jakob's side. We ended up by a wide, deep pool. Water was shooting up out of the middle of it in white spray and bubbles. I stuck my nose in and lapped up a little, just to see what it tasted like. *Yuck!* Something sour and chemical had spoiled this water completely. I shook my head hard.

Jakob chuckled. 'The fountain doesn't taste like your water bowl at home, huh? OK, Ellie.' He'd picked up a stick. 'Get it!'

Fetch! I loved Fetch! Jakob held the stick up over his shoulder and threw it hard. It landed right in the water.

Right in the water!

I bent my nose down and sniffed at the strange-smelling water. Then I dipped a paw in it. Cold! I jerked the paw back.

I wasn't a little puppy scared of my own water dish any more. But still, I didn't really like this. That was a *lot* of water. I knew what Jakob wanted, though. He wanted me to get the stick for him. He never liked to lose his sticks for long.

I put two paws in, expecting to support myself with my forelegs, but to my utter shock I didn't touch the bottom. I fell in the pool! Water flooded into my eyes and nose. Sputtering, choking, I scrabbled and clawed my way out of the pool in an utter panic, shaking myself off violently.

'Fetch! Get the stick, Ellie!'

Forget the stick. I wasn't going back in there, ever. Plunging under the surface of the water reminded me too much of my dream about the boy. What was his name? Ethan. In the water, sinking down and down. The fear from that dream haunted me now, strong as any real-life memory.

The fountain was cold. And worse, the water was constantly moving up and down, sloshing back and forth. It was dangerous. I didn't want to do this.

'The stick!' Jakob insisted.

You want a stick? I scampered across the lawn, jumping with both feet on a nice big stick. I picked it up and shook it to show Jakob how fun it was.

'Ellie, come!' he commanded sternly.

Oh-oh. I went to him with my tail lowered, dropping the new stick at his feet.

'You don't like water, huh?' Jakob had crouched down and was eyeing me. 'That could be a problem, you know. C'mon, Ellie, get the stick. You can do it. Go Swim.'

Swim? I couldn't do it, if Swim meant going in the water.

Jakob picked up the new stick and threw it, too, in the water. *Oh no!* 'Go on, Ellie. It's not that bad. Fetch!'

Why didn't he just throw the stick the other way? I

ran a few feet, to show him where I wanted him to throw it. *Come on, Jakob. This way! Throw the stick on the ground! The ground is so much nicer than the pool!*

But he didn't. He threw another stick into the fountain, and another. I whined a little, letting him know this was not a good idea. Water was not safe. People should not go into it. Dogs should not, either.

'OK,' Jakob said thoughtfully, staring at me. 'OK . . .'

And he jumped in.

One minute he was standing next to me; the next he was gone. He flopped forward in the water, made a few motions with his arms, and sank.

He sank! Just like that boy, Ethan!

I barked so Jakob would know to come up. I paced back and forth by the edge of the fountain. Jakob! Jakob had gone into the water!

He hadn't given me a command, but I knew what I was supposed to do. I was supposed to Fetch him, the way I was supposed to Fetch the sticks. I was supposed to go into the water.

I didn't want to. But Jakob was down there. I had to get him back!

The next thing I knew, I was in the water, too.

My paws seemed to know what to do – I paddled as best I could, and I was moving towards Jakob. But the water was every bit as awful as the first time. My coat got so heavy it was hard to keep moving. The strange-smelling stuff splashed in my eyes and surged into my mouth and nose. It stung! I couldn't smell Jakob. I couldn't smell *anything*. Panic was creeping up on me. It had been so long, and Jakob hadn't come up, and I couldn't Find him. Finding was my job; it was my Work; it was our Work. I was supposed to Find Jakob!

Bubbles from underneath me tickled my belly. I looked down, blinking hard. There he was! Jakob!

He surged up, grabbing hold of me. Somehow he could stand, the water up to his waist. He shook the water out of his face and laughed one of his short laughs.

'Good girl, Ellie. You did it. You came in after me! Good dog!'

He gave me a push back towards the edge of the fountain and heaved me out, following me. We sat there, dripping, and he patted me more, scratching my wet ears.

'Hey! Hey there!' Someone ran out to us, someone in dark clothes like Jakob's. 'No swimming in that fountain. What are you doing, letting your dog play around like that?'

'She's not playing,' Jakob said, unhooking something shiny from his belt and holding it up for the other man to see. 'She's working.'

5

I knew Jakob had been happy that I'd gone in the water. I was glad he was pleased, but I was also very relieved when we went back to our old park the next day. I liked Find a lot better than Swim.

Wally wasn't around; I was used to that by now. I looked up at Jakob, my ears alert for 'Find'. But Jakob did something new. He had carried an old coat with him from the truck, and now he held it out to me. 'Find, Ellie. Find!'

Find the coat? That was strange. The coat was right there over Jakob's arm.

Jakob moved the coat closer to me, so that I could smell it. I breathed in the aromas of the person who'd been wearing it. It wasn't Wally. The coat smelt of some-one else, another man. My nose picked up sweat, some-thing sweet that had spilt, coffee, smoke from those strange white sticks people liked to put in their mouths.

'Find, Ellie!'

I was still confused, but I sniffed around a little on the grass. Find usually started with smelling. And there it was – the same smell that was on the coat.

I remembered how I often found Wally's socks or his T-shirts and showed them to Jakob. This seemed to be the same sort of thing. Except that I was not supposed to find this coat and bring Jakob to it; I was supposed to find the person who had worn the coat.

Now that I knew what to do, it was easy. The trail was fresh and strong, and it wasn't hard to follow it along the grass, between two benches, under the trees – and there he was. A man in a yellow sweater and a brown hat, with one of those white sticks in his mouth. When I ran back for Jakob, he knew right away that I had something to Show and he followed me to where the man was still waiting. The man got up and shook Jakob's hand, and I heard Jakob thanking him after I got a good game of tug-on-a-stick.

The next day was even stranger. Jakob and I went back to the park, and he did nothing but look down at me. 'Find!' he said.

I sniffed. No smell of the man with the coat. No

smell of Wally. I looked up at Jakob. What did he want me to do?

He was watching me intently. 'Find!' he repeated. 'Find, Ellie!'

I went back to sniffing the ground, hoping that would give me more clues. There were a lot of interesting smells: the grass itself, the dirt beneath, places here and there where other dogs had peed, some popcorn that had been dropped, a trail where a raccoon had wandered past in the night, another where a rabbit had hopped by a few hours ago. Feet had crisscrossed this area, and so had paws. I sniffed harder.

'Sometimes I need you to look for any people you can, Ellie,' Jakob said. I looked at his face when I heard my name. 'OK? Find!'

At the command I lowered my nose.

There *was* one smell that was fresh and stood out: female, human, not too old. I followed the trail a few feet. She wore rubber shoes. She'd eaten something with cream cheese for breakfast. She'd gone this way. I looked back at Jakob, to see if he'd tell me I was doing this wrong. He stood still as I moved away from him, watching me with that look he only got when we were Working, as if I were the only thing in the world he could see.

I put my nose back to the ground, not quite sure if this was the right thing to do. Still, Jakob had told me to

Find. The easiest thing to Find around here was the track of the girl who'd eaten cream cheese. I started to follow her.

Her trail led me to a bench. I stopped and sniffed hard. She'd sat here for a little while; I could smell her shoes and her clothes, her skin and her hair. But she wasn't here now. So Find was not over yet.

I followed the girl's trail away from the bench, across a lawn with soft grass. Some young humans were throwing a ball there and shouting. I moved quickly across the soft grass, and a red ball rolled right in front of my nose. It would have been so easy to pick it up and run back with it to the boy who had thrown it. Jakob wasn't here to see me do it, and it would only be a minute or two of play. The ball was right there, just inches from my nose . . .

But what about the girl? I was supposed to Find her. Jakob had said so. I couldn't stop and play now. There wasn't time for that. This was Work. Play came later.

The girl's trail led me across a muddy path. Then it started to wind around the roots of trees. I jumped across a thick root that twisted like a snake, and there she was, sitting under a tree with a book on her lap.

She looked up at me and smiled, then looked down and turned a page.

I ran to find Jakob, dashing back across the lawn, running right through the game of catch, feeling a little worried. Was this right? Was this what he'd wanted me to do?

It seemed to be. 'Show me!' he said as soon as I reached him. And, 'Good dog!' when I brought him to the girl. 'Good dog, Ellie!'

'What are you doing?' asked the girl, putting her book down on her lap and staring at us.

'She's a search-and-rescue dog,' Jakob explained. 'She's training to find people.'

The girl smiled widely. 'And she found me?'

'That she did.' Jakob found a stick for me and we played around the little clearing. The girl didn't seem to know that it was her job to play tug-on-a-stick. (Wally always knew.) But I didn't care too much, so long as someone was willing to pull and wrestle with me.

Maybe the girl wasn't all that bright, but she was still nice. She laughed and put out her hand when I came near, and I hoped she might have some cream cheese to share. She didn't have any, but she scratched behind my ears. That was nice, too.

I didn't like the next person I Found quite as much. He was crouched in a bush with a pair of big, strange-looking glasses held to his eyes, and he smelt sour, as if he hadn't had a good bath in a while. Someone needed to spray him with a hose.

'Shoo!' he hissed at me when I Found him the first time, and when I brought Jakob to him he stood up and frowned as Jakob called me a good dog and let me tug him all around the bush with my stick.

'Do you mind playing with your dog somewhere else?' the man asked grumpily. 'You've scared off a scarlet tanager!'

'Sorry, sir,' Jakob said. I didn't know what was being said, but the man seemed unhappy and Jakob didn't seem too concerned about it.

We Found a lot of people in the days after that. Some were glad to see us; some were not. But Jakob always told me I was a good dog, no matter how the person I Found acted. This was what Work meant, I decided. I was supposed to Find people and take Jakob to them, so that he could decide whether they were the right people or not. That was his job. Finding them was mine.

I had been with Jakob about a year when he started taking me to a new place to Work. This place had a lot of people in it, most of them dressed like Jakob. They were friendly and called me by name, but they drew back respectfully when Jakob told me to Heel.

There were also some other dogs in this Work place. Jakob took me out back to a fenced-in pen. 'Here's your kennel, girl,' he said. Two other dogs were inside already, Cammie and Gypsy. Cammie was jet black and Gypsy was brown.

I stood still and let them sniff me all over when Jakob

opened the door and let me inside. Then it was my turn to sniff them. They smelt all right. Gypsy was about my age; Cammie was older. After he'd inspected me, Cammie settled down on the ground with a sigh, as if he didn't find a new dog all that interesting.

Gypsy, though, had a fuzzy green ball in her mouth. She put it on the ground and let it roll a few inches away. Then she snatched it up again. She looked at me.

Hmmmm. A ball. A ball was something I could play with. Why should Gypsy have the ball and not me?

I didn't let on how much I'd like to have a ball, too. But the next time Gypsy allowed the ball to roll away, I pounced. She raced me to it, but she wasn't fast enough. I had it now! Gypsy chased me all around the kennel, and Cammie groaned a little when we tore right past his nose. Then I let Gypsy have the ball again and it was her turn to chase me.

But when Jakob came out into the yard, I quickly dropped the ball and went to sit by the fence to watch him. Gypsy snatched the ball up, but she came over, too. Even Cammie sat up, and his ears were alert.

Was it time to Work?

It didn't seem to be. Jakob just looked at me and nodded. 'Getting on all right?' he asked, and then he scratched my ears through the wire fence before he left again.

That was how it was, in the kennel. When Gypsy

and I had time, we played while Cammie watched. But if a person walked into the yard, our games were over. We dashed to the fence, ready if the call to Work came.

Gypsy worked with a police officer named Paul, and they were gone a lot. But sometimes I saw them work in the yard. They did it all wrong! Gypsy just poked her nose in between boxes and into piles of clothing, even when it was obvious there wasn't a person hidden there. Worse, she'd alert Paul when she hadn't Found anyone! But he always called her a good dog anyway and pulled a little package out from wherever her nose had been pointed.

Cammie didn't bother to watch Gypsy. Probably he felt embarrassed for the poor dog. Cammie's person was named Amy, and they didn't go out much. When they did, though, they went fast. Amy would come and get Cammie and they'd leave at a run.

I didn't really understand what either of them was doing. But I knew it couldn't be as important as Find.

'Where you working this week?' Amy asked Paul once.

'Looking for drug smugglers out at the airport again, until Garcia comes off sick leave,' Paul told her. 'How's life on the bomb squad?'

'Quiet. I'm worried about Cammie, though. His scores have been a little off. I'm wondering if his nose is going.'

At the sound of his name Cammie raised his head, and I looked over at him.

'He's, what, ten years old now?' Paul asked.

'About that,' Amy answered.

I stood up and shook myself because I could sense Jakob coming. A few seconds later he walked around the corner. He and the other officers stood and talked while we dogs watched them, wondering why they didn't let us out into the yard to be with them.

Suddenly I felt a surge of excitement off Jakob. He spoke to his shoulder, in that same funny way humans sometimes held up boxes near their faces and talked into them. 'Ten-four. Unit Eight-Kilo-Six responding,' he said.

Amy ran over to our gate. Cammie jumped up, but Amy didn't call for him. She was looking at me. 'Ellie!' Amy commanded. 'Come!'

Jakob was running and I streaked past Amy, chasing him. In moments we were out of the yard and I was in the cage in the back of the truck. I found myself panting, picking up some of Jakob's excitement.

Something told me that whatever was happening, it was far more important than Find Wally.

6

Jakob drove us to a large, flat building. Several people were outside the front door, gathered into a circle. I could feel the tension in them as we pulled up. Jakob came around and petted me, but he left me in the truck. 'Good dog, Ellie,' he said absently.

I sat and watched him anxiously as he went up to the group of people. What was he doing? Why was he walking away from me? Weren't we going to Work? I knew I was supposed to wait patiently for him to give me a command, but it was hard. I whined a little.

Several of the people near Jakob spoke at once.

'We didn't notice her missing until lunch, but we don't have any idea how long she's been gone.'

'Marilyn's an Alzheimer's patient. Sometimes she

thinks she's back at her old house, or that she needs to go to the job she used to have. She won't remember enough to find her way back.'

'I don't understand how she got away with no one seeing.'

While I sat there in the truck, a squirrel climbed down the trunk of a tree and scurried around, trying to dig up food in the grass. I stared at it, astounded. Didn't it realize that I was a vicious predator? And that I was only ten feet away?

Jakob came back to the cage and opened the door. 'Heel!' he commanded, giving me no chance to teach the squirrel a lesson. It shot up a tree anyway and sat up there, chattering. I ignored it. Time to Work.

Jakob led me away from the people to a corner of the front yard. He held out two shirts that smelt of old sweat, of something sweet and flowery. I stuck my nose into the soft cloth, breathing in deeply. 'Ellie, Find!'

It was just like the park. I knew exactly what to do, and I took off, running past the knot of people. 'She wouldn't have gone that way,' someone said.

'Let Ellie work,' Jakob replied.

Work. I carried the sense memory of the clothing in my mind as I held my nose up to the air, moving back and forth to pick up the trail. A lot of people had walked across this yard. Dogs had been along the pavement. Cars had driven down the street. I could smell all of them, but none of those smells was the right smell. I couldn't Find.

Frustrated, I turned back to Jakob.

He could tell I was disappointed. 'That's OK, Ellie. Find.' He began walking down the street, and I leaped ahead. There were more lawns; I dashed up and down each one. Somewhere that smell, the one right smell, would be hidden. I'd discover it.

I turned the corner and slowed down. There it was! It was faint, just a hint, but it got stronger as I moved in the right direction. It was tantalizing me, coming to me . . .

I homed in on the right trail, and the smell was powerful now. There was no doubt. I had Found it. Forty feet in front of me, at the base of a clump of bushes, there was a burst of the scent, perfectly clear. I turned and ran back to Jakob, who had been joined by several police officers.

'Show me, Ellie!' Jakob said at once.

I took him back to the bushes. He bent, poking at something with a stick.

'What is it?' one of the officers asked, coming up behind Jakob.

'A tissue. Good dog, Ellie, good dog!' He offered me the stick and we wrestled with it quickly, but I could sense that we weren't done here. There was more Work.

'How do we know that's hers? It could have been dropped by anybody,' one of the police officers objected.

Jakob ignored him. He bent down so his face was near mine. 'OK, Ellie. Find!'

I followed the trail as it led away from the tissue. It went about two blocks, then turned right, getting stronger. At a driveway it made another sharp right turn and took me through an open gate.

And there she was, sitting on a swing, moving gently. Her small feet just brushed the ground. There was a real sense of happiness flowing from her, and she seemed glad to see me.

'Hello, doggy,' she said. Somehow her voice sounded far away, even though she was only a few feet from me.

I ran back to Jakob. His excitement surged the moment he saw me. He knew that I'd done my Work. I had Found her! But he waited until I reached him before he reacted. 'OK, Show me!' he urged.

I took him to the lady on the swing, and I felt his relief the moment he stepped through the gate. 'Are you Marilyn?' he asked gently.

She tipped her head to one side, looking at him. 'Are you Warner?' she replied.

Jakob spoke into the microphone at his shoulder, and soon we were joined by the other police officers. Jakob took me into the front yard. 'Good dog, Ellie!' he praised. He pulled a rubber ring out of his pocket and sent it bouncing across the lawn, and I jumped on it and brought it back, holding it out for him to grip and tug on. We played for about five minutes, my tail whipping the air the whole time.

Someone new arrived then and led Marilyn back up the street with an arm around her. We followed. I could feel the relief pouring off the people who came out to meet Marilyn, call out her name, and take her inside.

She'd been in some kind of danger, that faraway, gentle lady named Marilyn. I understood that now. By Finding her, Jakob and I had saved her.

As Jakob shut me in the cage in the back of the truck, I could feel the pride coming off him. 'Good dog, Ellie. You are such a good dog.'

It wasn't the adoration I used to feel from Georgia, but it was as close as Jakob could come. That was the first moment I really understood my purpose: not just to Find people, but to save them.

That was what Jakob and I did together; that was our Work. And it was what he cared about most.

The next day, our Work was back to normal. Wally was hiding on top of a skip full of all sorts of rubbish – some of it smelt delicious, some smelt awful, but I was still able to pick out the Wally smell. He couldn't fool me! When Work was done, Jakob stopped by a store and picked up some sweet-smelling flowers. To my surprise, we didn't head home.

Instead, we drove and drove and drove. It took so long that I got tired of holding my nose up to the wire mesh of my cage. Usually I loved the rush of smells that poured over me when I rode in the truck. It was hard to believe that, when I was just a puppy, I'd been frightened of it. I loved it now. The smells came and went so quickly that I couldn't tell them apart, but it felt wonderful just to let them wash over me.

But I got tired of that at last and lay down on the floor with my head on my paws, waiting for the trip to be over.

When Jakob came to let me out, there was a heaviness in him. Whatever was hurting him inside seemed stronger than ever. He even moved more slowly, as if his sadness were something heavy that he had to carry with every step.

I hopped down out of the truck. We were in a big yard filled with smooth stones that stuck up out of the soft grass.

Not sure what we were doing, I stayed close to Jakob as he walked away from the truck, carrying his flowers. Was this Work? I didn't think so. Jakob never felt this sad when we were doing Work.

Jakob stopped walking and knelt down. He put the flowers next to one of the stones. The pain inside him twisted so deeply that tears fell silently down his cheeks.

I nuzzled at his hand, worried about him. It wasn't

right, for Jakob to cry like this. Something needed to be done about it.

'It's OK, Ellie. Good dog. Sit.'

I sat. Since I couldn't Find Jakob, or rescue him, or do anything to help him, I just stayed next to him, feeling sad with him.

He cleared his throat. 'I miss you so much, honey. I just . . . sometimes I don't think I can get through the day knowing you're not going to be there when I get home,' he whispered hoarsely.

I lifted my ears at the word 'home'. *Yes,* I thought. *Let's go home. Let's leave this sad place.*

But Jakob didn't move, and he kept on talking.

'I'm on K-9 patrol right now, search and rescue. I've got a dog. Her name is Ellie, a one-year-old German shepherd.'

I wagged my tail.

'You'd like her, honey. I wish you could have met her. She's a good dog; she really is.'

I wagged harder, but Jakob didn't seem to notice me, even though he'd said my name and, 'Good dog.'

'We just got certified, so we'll be going out, now. I'll be glad to get off the desk. I've gained about ten pounds from all the sitting.' Jakob laughed, and the sound of it was so peculiar that it nearly made me whimper. It was such a sad, tortured little laugh, with no happiness in it at all.

We stayed there, hardly moving at all, for about ten minutes. Jakob seemed like one of the pieces of stone sticking up out of the ground, hard and cold and motionless. Slowly, the feeling I could sense in him shifted. It was less raw pain and more of a feeling sort of like fear.

'I love you,' Jakob whispered. Then he got up and walked away. I followed closely at his heels.

7

From that day forward, we spent more time away from the kennel. There were a lot of people out there who needed to be Found. Sometimes they were adults and sometimes children. Sometimes they were scared. Sometimes they were confused or, like Marilyn, not really aware that they were lost. But most were happy to see us.

Sometimes we would ride on aeroplanes or helicopters. 'You're a chopper dog, Ellie!' Jakob always told me when we took off. The first time the noise made me nervous, but after that I understood that aeroplanes and helicopters were something like the truck – they got us to where Work needed to be done. The humming that I could hear and even feel through the metal floor started to make me drowsy after a time or two, and I'd usually doze off. When I woke up, Jakob and I would go to Work.

One day Jakob took me in the truck to the biggest pond I'd ever seen. There were a lot of people there, but a man and a woman ran towards the truck when we pulled up, talking frantically before Jakob even let me out of the cage. The woman pulled a limp purple sweatshirt from a big bag over her shoulder, and Jakob held it down for me to smell.

'Can your dog really . . .' the woman began, sounding like she was about to cry. 'I mean, we're not even sure how long it's been. I thought for sure Charlotte was playing with a few other kids down by the water, and then when I looked up she wasn't there. They didn't even remember seeing her leave.' Now the woman was crying for real and the man put an arm around her.

'Ellie's very good,' Jakob said calmly. 'We just need to let her do her job. Find, Ellie!'

I sniffed the sweatshirt deeply. Sunscreen . . . salt . . . ketchup . . . a smudge of ice cream . . . strawberry-smelling shampoo . . . and little girl. Now I knew who I was searching for.

I put my nose down to the sand. It smelt . . . different. I'd tracked people across grass, dirt, pavements, and roads. But this was something new. Everything smelt damp and salty, and there was a strong, wet, powerful scent of seaweed in the air, threatening to swallow up the fragile smell of little girl.

And there were crisscrossing smells of people everywhere. They had been walking all over this sand, coming in and out of the water. I smelt rubber shoes and bare skin and food. So much food! Someone was grilling hot dogs. Jakob sometimes cooked those on the stove and let me have a taste. So delicious! It was hard to resist the temptation to lift my head up and take in a big breath of that lovely smell, but I kept my head down. I was Working.

I paced back and forth, making my way down towards the water. It was very strange water. The smell of salt from it was strong. I'd thought that the fountain Jakob had jumped into was big, but this – it was huge, and it *moved*. It growled, too, as though it were angry. I would rather have stayed far away from it, but the girl's trail was leading right towards it. I had to follow.

Then the water, to my surprise, swept up close to my paws! I'd been following the trail right across the sand, and all of a sudden the water rolled up to me and then back. The smell had been washed away. I jumped back in surprise.

'It's OK, Ellie,' Jakob said. He'd followed close behind me. 'Find.'

That wasn't fair, the water coming up to wash the smell away! Irritated, I set to Work harder. The trail must be somewhere. I found it again in less than a minute. The little girl had been wandering close to the water's edge. The water kept moving, trying to trick me, but every time I lost the trail I found it again. My nose stayed right down near the sand.

'Doggy! Doggy!' a high voice said, and little hands were patting me. A tiny boy grabbed at my fur and giggled. His hands were sticky with salty water and drips from an ice lolly, and ordinarily I would have licked them clean.

'Will he bite?' asked a woman nervously.

'She won't bite, but she's working,' Jakob said from behind me. 'Could you please—'

But I could already tell this wasn't the child I was supposed to Find. So I gently walked around him and kept going, moving quicker and quicker. Jakob was falling behind.

Something round landed in the sand beside me, and I looked up, startled. 'Fetch!' a teenage boy yelled. I nosed at the thing. It was hard and plastic and looked like it might be nice to chew, but it wasn't Work. I kept going.

The girl's smell left the water. I followed it up the sloping sand and felt it growing stronger. I looked up to see a playground with more young humans than I had ever seen running wildly around. They slid down slides and climbed up ladders, just as I had learned to do. But they didn't seem to treat it as seriously as Work should

57

be treated. They were playing, and making a lot of noise doing it.

The tracks of so many children crossed and criss-crossed the sand, and the smell I was following was buried. I paced back and forth, turning in a half circle. Where had it gone? I lifted my nose and tried the air. She was close; she must be close. I'd find the smell again if I just didn't give up.

And I did! There she was, sitting on a seesaw with a little boy at the other end. She flew up in the air, giggling, and then thumped down in the sand. I turned back to Jakob. 'Show me!' he said, looking at my face.

I dashed across the playground. 'Dog!' 'Doggy!' 'Can I pet your dog!' children called out as I ran. The girl thumped down in the sand, bouncing on her seat, as I came up to her.

Jakob followed me. 'Charlotte?' he said. 'Are you Charlotte?'

'Uh-huh.' The little girl looked up and laughed. 'I want to play at the playground!' she shouted happily. 'I want to stay!'

When Charlotte was back with her parents (her mother cried some more and Charlotte cried when her parents said she had to leave the playground and go home), Jakob snapped my leash on and scratched behind my ears. 'Want to play in the ocean, Ellie?' he asked.

He took me down to the water. It kept sneaking up and trying to get me wet. I jumped back and barked, and once I tried to bite the bubbly white water that swirled over my paws. Jakob actually chuckled a little. It was a happier sound than I had ever heard from him before.

He found a stick and tossed it in the shallow water. Cautiously, I waded out to get it. The water sloshed around my feet and brushed against the fur on my belly, but it wasn't as bad as I'd thought it would be. I felt anxious, though, worried Jakob might go out in the water and sink in it. The thought was frightening. I snatched the stick up, tasted salt and wood, and raced back to Jakob, splashing all the way.

For once, there was a real smile on his face. 'This is the ocean, Ellie. The ocean!' he told me, and threw more sticks until I was running in without any hesitation to get them, dashing in and out of the waves, wet from nose to tail. I was happy. Jakob was not going to sink – he remained safely on the shore, grinning. I felt that thing that had such a tight clench on Jakob's heart loosen, just a little, as we played.

8

Gypsy was not at the kennel the next day, but Cammie was. I tried to get him interested in a glorious game of I've Got the Ball and You Don't, but he just lay with his head on his paws, watching me tolerantly.

Then Jakob came out into the yard. 'Ellie!' he called.

I'd never heard such urgency in his voice. I dropped the ball at once and ran to the gate so that he could let me out. We were obviously going to Work, and Work sounded more important than ever.

Jakob hurried with me to the truck, and we drove. The tyres made screeching sounds that I could hear above the wail of the siren when we turned the corners. I had to lie down flat, my claws digging into the floor of my cage, to keep from sliding around.

When the truck jerked to a stop, I could see people gathered in a car park. That wasn't unusual. People often came to watch Jakob and me Work. But these people were more worried than I'd ever seen. One of them, a woman, was so afraid she couldn't stand up, and two people were holding her. Anxiety was rippling off Jakob, so strong it made the fur on my back stand up.

Jakob left me in my cage and ran past me to talk to the people. I waited, whining a little, very softly. Something was wrong, very wrong. The only way to make it better was to go to Work right away.

We were in a car park next to a big building with glass doors. The frightened woman reached into a bag and took out a soft, floppy toy. It had long ears like a rabbit, and most of the fur had been rubbed off.

'We've got the mall locked down,' somebody said.

Jakob came to the door of my cage and opened it. He handed me the floppy rabbit to sniff. 'Ellie, OK? Got it? I need you to Find, Ellie!'

Another little girl, like Charlotte. But different. She had her own smell, of course; all humans did. This one combined sweat and dirt and peanut butter and salt, soap that smelt like honey, cookie crumbs. I leaped out on to the hard black ground and tried to sort out all the smells around me.

The ground itself smelt bitter and somehow black,

just like it looked. Many feet had crossed it. There was a foul-smelling puddle of oil and a sharp stink of petrol. Someone had spilt a cup of coffee. I moved away from those smells, concentrating. I was looking for little girl.

I didn't notice that I'd moved out in front of a moving car until the driver hit the brakes with a squeal. 'Hey, what the—' I heard an angry voice say.

Behind me, Jakob held up something in his hand. 'Police dog!' he said sharply. 'Back your vehicle up!'

'OK, sorry,' the driver mumbled.

But I wasn't paying attention to that. The car wasn't important. I'd found the track of the girl who'd held the soft rabbit. But her scent was mixed with another, unfamiliar one. Strong . . . adult . . . male. I tracked them both, moving quickly, sure of myself.

'She's got it!' I heard Jakob call.

Then the smell vanished right where a car sat in the car park. The two people I'd been following had gone. They must have driven away in a different car, and then this one had pulled in to take its place.

I turned back to Show Jakob. But he wasn't happy, I could tell. Frustration and disappointment rose off him like a cloud. I cringed a little. Hadn't I done the Work right? He'd always been happy before.

'OK, good girl, Ellie. Good dog.' He pulled a rubber ring out of his pocket. But he played with me for only a minute or two, and I could tell that he was thinking about something else.

Jakob had called me a good dog, but I didn't feel like one. He wasn't happy. The Work wasn't right. Or maybe it wasn't done.

'We've tracked her to here,' Jakob told a man in a suit. 'It looks like she got into a vehicle and left. Do we have surveillance on the car park?'

'We're checking now. If it is who we think it is, though, the car's stolen,' the man answered.

'Where would he take her? If it's him, where would he go?' Jakob asked.

The man in the suit turned his head, squinting at the green hills we could see in the distance. 'Topanga Canyon. Or Will Rogers State Park.'

'We'll head up that way,' Jakob said. 'See if we can pick up anything.'

I was startled when Jakob put me in the front seat of the truck. He'd never let me be a front-seat dog before! But he wasn't doing it because he was in a good mood; I could tell. He was still tense, so I stayed focused as he started up the car. We passed by another car with two terriers in the back seat of a station wagon, and they yipped at me out of pure jealousy, because I was in the front seat and they weren't. I ignored them.

Jakob and I drove out of the car park, and he held the soft stuffed rabbit out to me. I sniffed it obediently, but I was confused. Hadn't I already done this? Didn't I do it right?

'OK, girl,' Jakob said. 'I know this is going to sound strange, but I want you to Find.'

I turned and stared at him in bewilderment. *Find? In the truck?*

Jakob drove slowly, quickly glancing at me and then returning his eyes to the road. I'd been told to Find, but I didn't know how. I couldn't put my nose to the ground and hunt for the little-girl smell on that soft rabbit. But I could—

I lifted my nose to the window. Smells were rushing past so quickly it was hard to sort them out. 'Good girl!' Jakob praised. 'Find! Find the girl!'

My nose was still filled with the smell of the girl from the toy. Then a breeze brought me that same smell from outside the window, still entwined with the man's. I looked over at Jakob. 'Good girl!' he said, stepping hard on the brakes. Behind us, cars honked. 'Got it, girl?' he asked intently. But the smell had gone.

'That's OK; that's OK, Ellie. Good girl,' Jakob said, and let the truck ease forward.

I understood now; we were Working from inside the truck. Instead of my legs moving over the ground, hunting a smell, the truck was doing the moving for me. I put my nose back to the window. Hot tar, fumes from the cars, a whiff of something disgusting and delicious from an overflowing bin, a greasy and salty smell of fried chicken from a restaurant, but none of those was right. I was straining, rejecting any- and everything except the smell from the toy.

I felt the truck tilt as we headed uphill. Disappointment was rising from Jakob; I could feel it.

'I think we've lost her,' he muttered. 'Nothing, Ellie?'

At my name, I turned and looked at him. Then I went back to my Work. The smells were changing. A sharp, tangy smell from the pine trees. Warm earth. Dry grass. But no little girl, not the one I was supposed to Find.

'Unit Eight-Kilo-Six, what's your twenty?' the radio squawked.

'Eight-Kilo-Six, we are proceeding up Amalfi.'

'Any luck?'

'We had something on Sunset. Nothing since.'

'Roger that.'

I barked.

I didn't normally bark when I caught a scent. But we were Working from the truck and Jakob was so worried; none of this was normal. When the smell rushed in through Jakob's window, filling up the cab of the truck, I couldn't hold back. My tail thumped against the seat. This was it! I'd Found the smell again; the girl's and the man's together!

The truck slowed. I kept my nose pointed into the

smell. Jakob eased to a stop. 'OK, which way, here, Ellie?' he asked.

I climbed across the seat and into his lap, shoving my face out of his window. 'Left on Capri!' Jakob shouted, his voice sharp with excitement. A few minutes later the truck started to bump. 'We're on the fire road!' Jakob yelled.

I was alert, focused dead ahead, while Jakob wrestled with the truck, trying to keep it on the narrow road. He pushed me back into the other seat, away from the smell. I whined a little in frustration. 'Sorry, girl, I have to drive,' Jakob muttered. 'Hold on, just hold on . . .'

Suddenly the truck thumped to a stop, facing a yellow gate. 'Be advised, we need the fire department up here,' Jakob said urgently. 'There's a gate.'

'Ten-four,' crackled the voice from the radio.

Jakob pushed his door open hard, and we both jumped out.

A red car was parked to one side of the rough dirt road, and I ran over to it. My ears were up; my nose was straining; everything in me was on alert. Jakob had his gun out. 'We've got a red Toyota Camry, empty; Ellie says it belongs to our man,' Jakob said shortly. Then he led me around to the back of the car, watching me closely. 'No indication anyone is in the trunk of the car,' he said.

'Roger that,' said the radio voice.

The smell from the car wasn't as strong as what was coming from the breeze. Below us, through the trees, there was a canyon. That was where we should go. That was where the girl was, the girl who needed to be Found.

A steep road on the other side of the yellow gate held the man's smell. His was stronger, smudged into the dust of the road. Hers was more delicate, drifting on the air. He'd carried her.

'Be advised, subject took the road down to the camp,' Jakob said. 'He's on foot.'

'Eight-Kilo-Six, hold and wait for back-up.'

Jakob didn't seem to be paying any attention to the voice as it came out of his walkie-talkie. 'Ellie,' he said to me, putting his gun back on his belt. 'Let's go and find the girl.'

9

Jakob was afraid.

I could feel the fear rising off him into the air, and it made me nervous. Jakob had been worried, sometimes, when we were Working. He'd been serious, always. But he'd never been scared before, not like this.

I galloped back to nudge his hand with my nose. I felt better if I could touch him. But I knew I couldn't stay right next to him. I needed to Find, needed to Work. That would make Jakob's fear go away.

The girl's scent, faint but clear, pulled me forward, down the slope of the road. The path curved and I lost sight of Jakob behind me. Ahead of me were a few buildings, scattered across green grass.

One of the buildings had steps leading up to a big porch. Up on the porch, a man had his back to me, working on the door with some kind of long metal tool. A little girl was sitting quietly on the steps, huddled back against the railings as if she were cold. But it wasn't a cold day. The sun was hot on my fur and I was panting.

I slowed down a little, heading across the grass at a trot. The girl's sad face brightened a little as she saw me. She sat up and held out her tiny hand.

The man whirled around, staring at me. My hackles rose when our eyes met, and I felt my lips pulling up to show my teeth. There was something dark inside him, something vicious and wrong. I didn't like the smell of him at all, and I didn't like seeing him so near the little girl.

The man jerked his head up, looking back along the road I'd come from.

I turned and ran back. 'Doggy!' the girl called after me.

My claws digging into the dirt, I sprinted back to Jakob, who was jogging steadily down the road after me. 'You got her,' he said, after one look at my face. 'Good girl, Ellie. Show me!'

He could run nearly as fast as I could. We both tore down the road towards the building. The little girl was still sitting there, looking confused. But the man was nowhere to be seen.

'Eight-Kilo-Six, victim is secured and unharmed,' Jakob panted into his walkie-talkie. 'Suspect fled on foot.'

'Stay with the victim, Eight-Kilo-Six.'

'Roger that.'

I could hear in the distance the *wap-wap-wap* of a helicopter blade beating the air and then the sound of footsteps running down the road behind us. Two police-men came around the bend, sweating.

'How are you, Emily?' one of them said, running up to the girl. He was careful not to touch her, and he knelt down, bringing his face closer to hers. 'Are you hurt?'

'No,' said the little girl. She picked at a flower on her dress.

'Is she all right? Are you OK, little girl?' A third police officer had come running, slower than the other two. He was panting for breath, and he put his hands on his knees. He was larger than the other two, both taller and heavier. I smelt ice cream on his breath.

'Her name is Emily,' the first policeman said.

Jakob had been standing close to me, watching. The little girl looked up at him, and a shy smile touched her face. 'Can I stroke the doggy?' she asked.

I felt Jakob's relief, the worst of the fear vanishing in the warm sun. That's how I knew I'd done the Work right, even though it had been strange, trying to Find in the truck. I wagged my tail.

'Yes, sure,' Jakob said kindly to Emily. 'Then we've got to go back to work.'

My ears perked up at the word 'work'. Emily stroked my head and smiled. She wasn't scared any more, either. I licked her fingers quickly.

I could still feel a sternness in Jakob, even while he smiled down at Emily. We weren't finished. Somehow I knew it.

'OK, I'll . . . go with you,' said the big policeman. He was still breathing hard. 'John, you guys . . . remain here with the girl. Watch that he doesn't circle back around.'

'If he were close, Ellie would tell us,' Jakob said. I looked up at him. Were we ready? I was ready. Was it time?

'Find!' Jakob said. I leaped ahead into the bushes.

The brush was thick in spots, the soil underneath sandy and loose. I could track the man easily, though. The trail was fresh. He was headed steadily downhill.

The smell was sharp and strong in a stand of tall grass. I ran back to Jakob. 'Show me!' he said, and followed. I took him to the grass and to the iron rod hidden there, coated with the man's unpleasant scent.

Jakob and I had to wait more than a couple of minutes for the other policeman to catch up with us. 'I fell . . . couple of times,' he gasped. I could smell his embarrassment and the thick sweat dripping off him.

'Ellie says he was carrying this crowbar,' Jakob reported tensely. 'Looks like he dropped his weapon.'

'OK, now what?'

'Find!' Jakob commanded.

I dashed ahead, leaving the two men to follow. The man's scent was painted on bushes and hanging in the air, and it wasn't long before I could hear him scuffling through the leaves and the rough grass. I ran more quickly. The breeze from ahead grew damp, bringing me his smell more strongly.

I pushed through a thorny bush into a little clearing. The air was moist from a tiny stream, and the trees lifted their limbs high overhead, letting shade fall gently on the ground. He saw me and ducked behind one of those trees, just like Wally used to do. But Wally had never fooled me, and this man with the dark, bitter smell could not fool me, either.

I turned and ran back to Jakob. 'Show me!' he said.

I stayed close to Jakob as he pushed his way through brush and saplings back to where I'd left the man. Jakob and I stepped out into the little clearing. I could hear the stream trickling over the stones.

I knew where the man was hiding; I could smell his fear and his hate and his angry scent. I led Jakob towards the tree.

The man stepped out into the sunlight.

I heard Jakob shout, 'Police! Freeze!'

The man raised his hand, and there was a noise as sharp as a thunderclap.

Just a gun. I knew about guns; Jakob had shown me. Guns were OK. Noise couldn't hurt me. Noise could not hurt anybody.

But I sensed a flash of pain from Jakob, and he fell to the ground. I smelt blood, warm and salty, and I heard his gun clatter away over roots and rocks.

The man took another step forward, his arm still out, the gun still pointed at Jakob and at me. I sensed the man's pleasure, saw his gloating smile. I didn't know how, but somehow this man had hurt Jakob. He'd used the gun to make that noise, and now Jakob was on the ground.

Behind me, Jakob gasped for breath.

I didn't growl; I just lowered my head and charged. The gun made its terrible noise two more times, and then I had the man's wrist in my mouth. His weapon fell with a soft thump into the dust. It couldn't make that loud sound now, the sound that could hurt people, that had hurt Jakob so badly.

The man screamed at me, and I held on, shaking my head violently, as if he were my prey. My teeth broke his skin and tore into the muscles of his arm. His foot smacked into my ribs, but I did not let my jaw loosen.

'Let go!' he yelled.

'Police! Freeze!' shouted another voice. It was the big policeman, shoving his way out from behind a bush.

'Get the dog off me!'

'Ellie, it's OK. Down, Ellie. Down!' the other police-man commanded. I let go of the man's arm and he fell to his knees. His eyes met mine. I could feel his pain but also his cunning. He was happy in some odd, twisted way, even though he was on the ground with his arm bleeding.

I didn't trust him, and I growled, warning him. He thought he was going to get away with something.

'Ellie, Come,' the policeman ordered.

I had always obeyed Come, ever since Jakob had taught me the words with treats in his pocket. I backed up, my eyes never leaving the bleeding man.

'Dog ripped off my arm!' the man shouted. He waved at something behind and to the left of the policeman. 'I'm over here!' he called out.

When the policeman turned quickly to see what was behind him, the man lunged, scooping up his gun and leaping to his feet. I barked, quickly, loudly, and my body tensed to spring.

The man I'd Found fired his gun and the noise made my ears hurt. But the big policeman was already turn-ing. His gun made its own noise twice, and the other man fell to the ground, just as Jakob had done.

'Cannot believe I fell for that one,' the big policeman muttered, pointing his gun at the man while he lay on the ground. The policeman took a few cautious steps forward and kicked the other gun away into a patch of grass.

'Ellie? You OK?' Jakob asked faintly.

'She's OK, Jakob. Where were you hit?'

'Gut.'

I'd already left the man I'd Found. He wasn't a threat any more; I could tell. And Jakob needed me. I ran to his side but lay down a foot or so away. Then I crawled forward carefully so I could nudge at his hand with my nose. I sensed I had to be very careful, not to touch him too much.

Jakob's hand didn't lift to scratch my ears, the way it always had. I licked it and whined. I could feel the pain deep inside him, feel it working its way through his body. The smell of the blood was powerful; I could hardly smell anything else.

'Officer down, suspect down. We're . . .' The policeman looked up at the sky. 'We're under some trees down the canyon. Need an air ambulance for the officer.'

'Who is the officer?' came the voice from his walkie-talkie.

'Eight-Kilo-Six. We need some help down here *now*.'

I didn't know what to do. Jakob had been afraid before, but now he seemed calm. I wasn't, though. I was panting and trembling with fear. I'd done my job; I'd Found the girl, and she was safe. I'd Found the man. That was right, wasn't it? That was what I was supposed to do?

But the man had hurt Jakob. That wasn't what should happen. Finding people was supposed to mean saving them. Now Jakob was the one who needed saving. I didn't know how, though. I was here, right beside him. But that wasn't enough. It wasn't what he needed.

The big policeman knelt next to Jakob. 'They're on their way, bro. You just got to hang on, now.'

I felt the worry in his voice. Gingerly, he opened up Jakob's shirt to get a look inside. The shock of fear that went through him made me whimper.

Soon I could hear crashing and stumbling as several people ran towards us. They knelt by Jakob, pushing me aside, and began working on him. I smelt sharp chemicals, and I saw them pressing cloths where there was the most blood.

'How's Emily?' Jakob asked them faintly.

'Who?'

'The little girl,' the big policeman explained. 'She's fine, Jakob. You found her. You saved her. Everything's OK.'

More people arrived, and they lifted Jakob on to a strange, flat bed and started to carry him up the canyon. I ran right beside him. Ahead of us, I heard the familiar sound of a helicopter motor stirring to life.

The policeman who'd been with us held on to my collar as the people put Jakob on the helicopter. The blades started spinning faster and faster, whipping dust and leaves through the air, and the helicopter rose slowly into the sky.

I wrenched myself free from the policeman's hand and ran after the helicopter, barking. It rose up and up and I circled beneath it, dancing on my hind legs, barking in frustration. I was a chopper dog! Why hadn't they let me get on? I needed to go with Jakob!

But the helicopter didn't come back. After a while Amy came to get me. She talked to the big policeman for a while and then clipped a leash on my collar and took me for a truck ride. The cage I was riding in was filled with Cammie's scent.

Amy took me back to the kennel at the police station, calling Cammie to her as I went in. Gypsy was nowhere to be seen.

Amy put the leash on Cammie and scratched behind my ears before she shut the door, leaving me in the kennel alone.

'Someone will check on you, and we'll figure out where you're going to live, Ellie. You be a good dog. You are a good dog,' Amy said.

10

I curled up on my bed in the kennel, my head whirling with fear and confusion. I did not feel like a good dog.

I'd done my Work. But now Jakob was gone and I was sleeping all night long at the kennel, instead of in my own bed next to Jakob's big one. It felt like I was being punished. But for what?

For biting the man with the gun? Biting people was not part of Finding them; I knew that. And now Jakob was hurt. The memory of his pain and the smell of his blood made me whimper as I lay there.

I remembered how I'd felt when I was a puppy and Jakob had left me in the apartment. I'd been worried each time, but Jakob had always come back. The thought made me feel better. Jakob would come back. All I had to do was wait.

The next few days were even more confusing. I lived in the kennel. A few times a day one of the police officers would come and let me out into the yard, but they never had Work for me to do and they would put me back into the kennel quickly and hurry away.

Amy talked to me and played with me a little, but she and Cammie were gone a lot of the time. Sometimes Gypsy wanted to play I've Got the Ball and You Don't, but I did not feel like it. Mostly I sat at the gate, waiting.

Slowly Jakob's smell faded from the yard. Even when I concentrated, I could not locate him. If I was supposed to Find him, I would not be able to. The thought made me bark anxiously until Amy came to let me out and pet me and talk to me.

I couldn't understand her words, but I felt a little better. That day I played with Gypsy and got the ball away from her twice.

A few days later, Amy brought her lunch out to a table in the yard. Cammie and I were in the kennel together, but all he wanted to do was nap. He wasn't interested in playing, even when I showed him a rubber bone one of the police officers had given me.

I didn't understand what Cammie's job was. Why would anyone want to have a nap dog?

Cammie was interested in Amy's lunch, however. She let us both out, and he walked over to the table and sat down heavily at her feet. He sighed, as if he had many serious problems that could only be cured with a bite of her ham sandwich.

A woman came out and joined Amy, sitting down at the other side of the table.

'Hi, Maya,' said Amy.

Maya had dark hair and dark eyes and was tall for a woman. Her arms looked strong. Her trousers smelt faintly of cats. She sat down and opened a little box, then took a fork out of it and began chomping on something spicy. 'Hi, Amy,' she said. 'Hello, Ellie.'

Maya didn't say hello to Cammie, I noticed. I liked that. I liked her. I liked Amy, too, but Amy belonged to Cammie. She wasn't my human, the way Jakob had been.

When would Jakob come back? He'd been gone such a long time. Maya, though, was right here. And she smelt good. So did her food. I moved closer to her. She petted me, smoothing down the fur on my head. I caught a whiff of soap and tangy tomatoes on her skin.

'Did you put in your paperwork?' Amy asked.

'Fingers crossed,' Maya replied.

I lay down and gnawed at my rubber bone. Maybe Maya would see how much fun I was having and decide to coax my attention back by offering me a bite of her lunch.

'Poor Ellie. She's got to be so confused,' Amy said.

I looked up. *Lunch?*

'You sure you really want to do this?' Amy asked.

Maya sighed, and I could feel some tension coming off her. 'I know it's hard work. But what isn't, you know? I'm just getting to that point; it's the same old thing every day. I'd like to try something new, do something different for a few years. Hey, you want a taco? My mum made them. They're really good.'

'No thanks.'

I sat up. *Taco?* I wanted a taco!

Maya wrapped up the rest of her lunch, as if I weren't even there. 'You people in K-9 are all in such good shape. Losing weight is so hard for me . . . you think I can hack it?'

'What? No, you're fine! Didn't you pass the physical?'

'Sure,' Maya said.

'Well, there you go.' Amy stuffed her rubbish into a little paper sack. 'I mean, if you want to run with me, I usually go to the track after work. But I'm sure you'll be great.'

I felt Maya calm down, just a little, as if Amy's words had been what she needed to hear. 'I sure hope so,' she said. 'I'd hate to let Ellie down.'

I decided that, no matter how often they said my name, this conversation wasn't going to involve anything to eat. I sprawled out in the sunshine with a sigh, wondering how much longer it would be before Jakob came back and we could go to Work again.

Maya came and ate lunch in the yard a few times after that. Then one day she came into the yard without any food. She was happy and excited; the feelings were floating off her, and she was smiling. She clipped on my leash and took me for a car ride.

'We're going to work together, Ellie. Isn't that great? You won't have to sleep in the kennel any more. I bought a bed for you; you can sleep in my room.'

There were some words in there that I knew: 'Ellie', 'kennel', 'bed'. And, of course, 'Work.' But none of what she had said made any real sense. We weren't going to Work; I could tell just from Maya's voice and the lack of tension in her body. So why was she talking about it?

I didn't mind that much, though. I was happy to go somewhere, anyway, after so many days in the same place. Plus, Maya let me ride in the back seat of her car. I stuck my nose out the window, blissfully drinking in the smells of everything that was not the kennel.

Maya parked in the driveway of a small house. As soon as she took me in the door, I knew it was hers. Her smell was painted everywhere. Alongside it was the odour of cats. That was a disappointment.

I carefully inspected every corner of the house. There was an orange cat sitting on a chair at the table. She watched me warily with cold eyes. When I came closer, tail wagging, she opened her mouth wide to show me her teeth and gave an almost silent hiss.

'Stella, be nice. That's Stella. Stella, this is Ellie; she lives here now.'

Stella yawned and turned her head to lick the fur on her back, as if I weren't even worthy of being noticed. I would have taught her a lesson or two, but a flash of grey-and-white movement out of the corner of my eye drew my attention.

'Tinker? That's Tinkerbell; she's shy.'

Another cat? I followed Maya into the bedroom. There a third cat, a heavy brown-and-black male, sauntered out from under the bed and sniffed at me. I could smell his fish breath.

'And that's Emmet,' Maya told me.

Stella, Tinkerbell and Emmet. Why on earth would one woman want three cats?

Tinkerbell stayed under the bed for the rest of that evening, thinking I couldn't smell her there. When Maya poured some food for me into a bowl, Emmet came into the kitchen and stuck his nose into my dinner. Then he lifted his head and walked away, as if he didn't even care that I was eating and he wasn't. I made sure to lick the bowl clean. No cats were getting any of my food. Stella stayed on the chair and watched me without blinking.

After dinner Maya let me out into her tiny yard.

'Good girl, Ellie!' she said after I'd done what I was supposed to do. Some humans seem to get excited when they notice dogs peeing in the yard; I guessed that Maya was one of them.

Maya made her own dinner, which smelt pretty good. Stella seemed to think so, too, because she jumped right up on the table and waltzed around, like a bad cat! I couldn't believe her lack of manners. Maya didn't even scold her. I suppose Maya thought cats weren't even worth training. After spending the afternoon with these three, I pretty much agreed with her.

After dinner we went for a walk on the leash. There were a lot of people out in their yards, adults and children of all ages. All the different smells made me restless. I hadn't done any Work in a long time, and I was getting impatient. I wanted to run, to Find, to save people. Without meaning to, I began to pull against the leash that Maya held.

Maya seemed to understand. 'Want to run a little, girl?' she asked, and she began to trot alongside me.

I sped up, sticking right by Maya's side, as Jakob had taught me. Before long she was breathing hard and I could smell sweat breaking out from her pores. Inside the houses we passed, dogs starting barking, jealous that we were running and they were not.

But all of a sudden Maya stopped. 'Whew!' she panted. 'OK, we're going to need to spend more time on the treadmill, that's for sure.'

I was disappointed. No more running? But I turned obediently when Maya tugged on the leash, and we headed back home.

It seemed that Maya's house really was home now.

I began to understand it, that night. I stretched out on the living room rug while Maya took a bath and changed into different, softer clothing. Then she called me into her bedroom. 'OK, lie down here, Ellie. Good girl,' she said, patting a dog bed.

I knew about dog beds. I curled up in it at once, and Maya praised me before she lay down in the big bed above me. But I was confused.

Would I be staying here for a while? I remembered how I had once lived in the basement with Mother and my littermates and then I had lived with Jakob. Had things changed again? Did I live here now?

But what about Jakob? Wasn't he going to come back this time? I had waited patiently. He'd always come back before. But this time – was it going to be different?

And what about my Work? How could I do Work without Jakob?

The next morning I found out.

Maya took me in her car, and we went back to the park where I had gone so often with Jakob. Wally was there, and he greeted me like an old friend. Belinda had come, too. She smiled and scratched my ears in just the right way. Then she waved and walked off into the woods while Wally stayed to talk to Maya.

I knew a lot of the words he used when he talked with her: 'Come' and 'Find' and 'Show me'. But he wasn't saying them to me, so it didn't seem as though I was supposed to do anything. I lay down and put my head on my paws, sighing with impatience. Wasn't I going to get to do any Work?

Then Maya said something exciting. 'Ellie, Find!'

I jumped up. *Yes! Work! At last!*

I quickly sniffed the grass and picked up a trail; it was Belinda's. She smelt like coffee, and a tangy perfume, and sugar from the doughnut she'd been eating. I followed the trail, running quickly just for the pleasure of it. Wally and Maya followed.

Belinda was sitting inside a car. If she'd been hoping to fool me that way, no luck! I circled back to Maya.

'See now; see how she looks?' Wally said. 'She found Belinda. You can tell by her expression.'

I waited impatiently for Maya to tell me to Show, but she and Wally were too busy talking. I could have barked with impatience, but I knew better. It was hard to wait, though. It had been so long since I'd Found anyone. I wanted to finish the job!

'I'm not sure,' Maya said. 'She doesn't look much different than the other times she came back.'

'Look at her eyes, the way her mouth is tightened,' Wally told Maya. 'Her tongue's not out. See? She's on alert; she has something to show us.'

At the word 'show' I started to lunge forward, but then I pulled myself back. It hadn't really been a command. But why not? Why weren't we doing our jobs?

'So now I tell her to show?' Maya asked.

I whined. *Quit teasing me!* Were we Working or not?

'Show!' Maya finally called.

Yes! At last! I tore off across the park, and Maya hurried along behind me. Belinda came out of the car laughing when we Found her. 'Such a good dog, Ellie,' she told me.

'Now you play with Ellie,' Wally said to Maya. 'It's important; it's her reward for such hard work.'

Maya took something out of her pocket – the rubber bone from the kennel. I leaped to grab it with my teeth. She laughed as she tugged on the bone and I pulled back, swinging her in a circle on the grass.

It was different from the times Jakob had played with me. He'd done it because he had to; it was a part of Work. Maya was smiling even when I pulled the bone out of her hand and she almost fell to the grass. 'You're so strong, Ellie!' she gasped, and laughed some more. 'Good girl, Ellie!' She petted me and scratched my neck and we played a little more tug-of-war with the bone before we got back to Work.

It was different, doing Work with Maya. But it was still Work, and that was the most important thing.

11

It wasn't just Work that was different with Maya. Almost everything about her was different from my old life with Jakob.

There were all the cats, for one thing. She also knew many more people than Jakob did. Most nights she went to a larger home with lots of people and a wonderful-smelling woman named Mama. Mama was always cooking; that's why she smelt so good. There were little children running around playing with each other every time Maya and I went for a visit.

The older children called, 'Ellie, Ellie! Ellie's here!' and almost forgot to say hello to Maya. The boys threw balls for me, which I patiently brought back. The girls put hats on me and laughed so hard they had to hold on to each other to stay on their feet. And the very small ones crawled on me and over me and poked fingers in my eyes.

I didn't mind too much, though. I remembered how my brothers and sisters and I used to play with Bernie. These little ones were like puppies; I understood that. They didn't know how to play correctly yet, and you just had to be patient while they learned.

When I got tired of having my fur pulled, I'd just shake myself gently to push them off, and go and sit under the table in the kitchen. Mama would be in the room, stirring things in bowls or tasting things in pots, and there was almost always something tasty that needed to be licked up off the floor. I loved the kitchen.

At her own house, Maya had a neighbour named Al who liked to come over and talk to her. There was a word he said so often that I began to recognize it. The word was 'help'.

'Do you need help carrying those boxes, Maya?' he'd ask. 'Do you need help fixing your door?'

'No, no,' Maya would say.

'Did you get a new dog?' Al asked one day, not long after I'd come to live with Maya. He bent down and scratched me behind the ears in a way that made me love him instantly. Not everybody scratches right, just hard enough and in the perfect place. Al did. I leaned against him happily so he wouldn't stop. He smelt of papers and ink and coffee and nervousness.

'Yes,' Maya said, talking a little more quickly than she usually did. 'She's the department search-and-rescue dog.' Maya's skin was growing warm, and her palms had started to sweat. This always happened when Al came over and said 'help'. But I could tell she wasn't frightened of him. It was odd. Still, as long as Al kept scratching I didn't care too much.

'Do you need help training your new dog?' Al asked.

I knew they were talking about me. I wagged my tail.

'No, no,' Maya said. 'Ellie has already been trained. We need to learn to work together as a team.'

I wagged extra when I heard the words 'Ellie' and 'work'.

Al straightened up and stopped scratching. 'Maya, you . . .' he started to say.

'I should probably go,' Maya mumbled.

'Your hair is very pretty today,' Al blurted.

The two of them stared at each other, both so anxious it felt as if something bad was going to happen any minute. I looked around to see if something was going to attack us. But I couldn't see anything more threatening than Emmet, who was staring at us through a window, probably jealous that I got to be Outside and he didn't.

'Thank you, Al,' Maya said. 'Would you like . . . ?'

'I'll let you go,' Al said.

'Oh.'

'Unless . . .'

'Unless . . . ?'

'You . . . do you need help with anything?'

'No, no,' Maya said.

Al nodded and walked away. I could feel Maya's sadness, and I pushed myself closer to her, so that she could scratch my ears, too.

Maya and I went to Work almost every day. Sometimes we Found Wally and sometimes Belinda. On some days a few of the older children from Mama's house came, too. That was fun; they were always so happy to be Found, and called me a good dog over and over, and wanted to play tug-on-a-stick until Maya, laughing, told them I had to do more Work.

Maya was much slower than Jakob, though, panting and sweating from the moment we started running. I learned not to be impatient when I circled back for her and all she could do was put her hands on her knees for a few moments. Once, after I had Found Wally and come back to Show Maya, she was crying. A burst of frustration and helplessness swept over her, and tears came with it.

I stared at her, waiting for her to be ready. I knew she was sad, but I couldn't comfort her now. We were Working. She knew it, too. She wiped her face quickly.

'OK, Ellie. Show me!'

I took her to where Wally was sitting on a big rock by the stream. We all went back to a picnic table together, and Wally took cool, wet cans out of a plastic box and handed one to Maya. Maya put a little bowl down on the grass for me and filled it with water from a bottle. I slurped it up and lay down in the shade of the table.

I could feel Maya's worry, and I put my head on her foot.

'We're not good enough to get certified, are we?' Maya asked. I heard her put her elbows on the table and sigh.

'Ellie's about the best dog I've ever seen,' Wally said, a little cautiously. He sounded nervous.

'No, I know it's me. I've always been heavy.'

'What? No, I mean . . .' Wally was actually scared now. I sat up, wondering what the danger was this time.

'It's OK. I've actually lost some weight. Like four pounds.'

'Really? That's great! I m-m-ean, but you weren't fat or anything,' Wally stammered. I smelt the sweat popping out on his forehead. 'You could, I don't know, maybe go to the track, that would help, or something?'

'I do go to the track!'

'Right! Yes!' Wally was so anxious I whined a little. 'Well, OK, I should go now.'

'I don't know,' Maya went on sadly. 'I didn't realize

there would be so much *running*. It's a lot harder than I thought it would be. Maybe I should resign, let somebody take over who's in better shape.'

'Hey, why don't you talk to Belinda about this?' Wally said desperately.

Maya sighed and Wally, full of relief, got up and left. I lay back down next to Maya. Whatever horrible danger had been lurking seemed to have gone away.

The next day Maya and I didn't Work. She put on some soft new shoes, grabbed my leash, and took me to a long road that ran along the sand next to that big pond, the ocean, where I had found the little girl named Charlotte.

Dogs were everywhere, but even though Maya didn't give me any commands, I sensed that this was a new kind of Work. So I ignored their barking and dashing back and forth. Maya and I ran and ran together down that road, further than we had ever run before. I sensed a new kind of determination in her. She kept going as the sun rose steadily in the sky, and I kept pace beside her.

It was the longest run we'd ever taken together. It went on and on until I felt Maya's body fill up with pain and exhaustion. Then, at last, she turned back.

The return trip was just as determined. We stopped a few times, and Maya let me drink out of taps set into the concrete next to very smelly buildings. Then Maya would start to run again. Each time she went a little slower, but she kept going.

At last the car park came into view ahead of us, and Maya slowed to a walk. 'Oh my,' she whispered.

By the time we got to the truck, she was limping.

We were both panting pretty hard. Maya sat down on the back of the truck and drank half a bottle of water, then bent down to hang her head between her legs. Then she threw up the water she'd just drunk.

I came and put my head on Maya's knee, sad that she was hurting so much. She was too tired to even lift a hand to stroke my head.

'You OK?' a young woman passing by asked. She was sweating from her run but breathing easily. Maya nodded without even looking up.

The next day we did Find again. Maya groaned as she eased herself out of the car and walked to the picnic table. I sat at her feet, waiting eagerly for the command.

Maya sighed. 'Find, Ellie,' she said. Her voice was low and sad.

I leaped forward, sniffing the ground eagerly. I couldn't smell Wally anywhere, but I caught Belinda's trail easily. She'd walked over this ground not long ago at all. It would not be hard to Find her

I heard Maya groan, and I hesitated and looked back. Maya was walking as if every step hurt. And she was so slow! I ran forward, following Belinda's trail under some trees. She'd forced her way between two bushes, leaving her scent all over the leaves. I followed. Then I stopped. I shoved my body back between the bushes and ran to Maya.

She looked down at me in surprise. 'Ellie? Having trouble, girl? Find!'

No, I wasn't the one having trouble. Maya was limping after me, determined, but she couldn't go fast at all and I could tell from how she was walking how much her muscles hurt. I didn't want to get too far ahead. She might not be able to catch up with me, and then how could I Show Belinda to her?

I trotted along the trail. It was hard to slow down. The trail was clear and I wanted to charge ahead, to Find Belinda as quickly as possible. But I kept my pace slow, so that Maya could keep up. I heard her push through the bushes behind me, and I dashed to her side, glanced up at her, and turned back to the trail on the ground.

Belinda had waded through a little stream and walked along it, but I found her easily on the other side and kept going. Maya plodded grimly through the water behind me. I dashed up a little hill and paused on the top to be sure Maya was following. When I was sure that she was, I ran ahead through a stand of tall grass, Belinda's scent growing stronger with every step I took.

I burst out of the grass, and there Belinda was,

stretched out under a tree. Her head was leaning back against the trunk. Her eyes were closed.

I ran back to Maya. She was making her way slowly up the hill. 'Oh, Ellie, good,' she panted when she saw me. 'Show me!'

I walked up the hill, keeping just a few feet ahead of Maya, glancing back over my shoulder often to be sure she was still with me. We pushed our way through the tall grass and Found Belinda, asleep under the tree.

Maya took a few deep breaths. 'Good dog. You are such a good dog, Ellie,' she whispered to me, and she sniffed hard. Then she cleared her throat. Belinda woke up with a start. She glanced at her wrist and I felt a little shock of surprise come off her.

'Just . . . had an off day,' Maya said. Belinda nodded and smiled and got to her feet.

That night Maya went to take a bath while I stayed in the living room. Tinkerbell was, as usual, hiding from the world. Stella was in the bedroom, checking out my bed; I could tell from the smell that she'd even tried sleeping there while Maya and I were at Work.

'Ellie!' Maya called. 'Ellie, come!'

Only her head was sticking up out of the water in the bathtub. I sniffed curiously at the warm bubbles and lapped up a little of the water, but it was terrible. I shook my head to chase the taste away.

Emmet sat on the bath mat, licking himself and

waiting for something to happen that he could ignore.

Maya reached out a wet hand and stroked my head. 'I'm sorry, Ellie.' Her voice was low and sad. 'I'm just not good enough. I just can't keep up with you in the field. You're such a good dog. You need someone who can handle you.'

I wagged when I heard that I was a good dog. Usually people were happy when I was good. But Maya's sadness did not change. She looked lonely, in the water all by herself. Would she be happier if I got into the tub with her?

I put my paws up on to the edge. Maya was already lying on the bottom, so she couldn't sink, which made it look like a lot more fun than jumping into the fountain after Jakob or even splashing in the ocean. Emmet stopped licking himself and looked at me without any of the proper respect. I'm not sure he ever understood that I could eat him in two bites, if I wanted to. Just because I didn't want to was no reason for him to get snooty about it.

Then he waltzed out of the room with his tail in the air, as if he were daring me to chase him down and do something about the fact that this house had too many cats.

'Tomorrow, I have a surprise for you, Ellie,' Maya said.
Well, OK. I'd gone this far . . .

I heaved my back legs up and splashed into the tub

right on top of Maya, sinking down through the clouds of bubbles. Warm water sloshed over the edge and on to the bathroom floor.

'Ellie!' Maya burst into laughter, her delight blowing out the sadness like a candle.

12

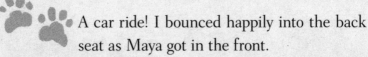A car ride! I bounced happily into the back seat as Maya got in the front.

We couldn't be going to Work, because Maya was happy. Lately she was never happy about Work. Today there was a little buzz of excitement coming off her, and it made me excited, too. I stuck my nose out of the window, drinking in the smells that rushed past, and my tail smacked the seat of the car as I wagged.

But it wasn't until Maya stopped the car and opened the door that I realized where I was.

Jakob's apartment!

I ran ahead of Maya, bounding up the stairs and barking at the door. I never would have done that when I lived with Jakob. But I was so happy that I couldn't help myself. Jakob! I was going to see Jakob again!

I could smell him inside and hear him moving to the door. He opened it and I barrelled into him, leaping and twisting joyfully. It had been so long since I'd seen him or smelt him or heard his voice!

'Ellie! How are you, girl? Sit!' he commanded.

I dropped my bottom on to the floor, but it didn't want to stay there.

'Hi, Jakob,' Maya said from the doorway.

'Come on in, Maya,' he answered.

Jakob walked towards a chair, and I bounced up to walk with him. He moved more slowly than he used to, and he held on to the back of the chair as he eased himself into it.

I put my head on his knees. I would have climbed into his lap, even, just as I'd done with Maya in the tub. But I knew better. Jakob wouldn't allow that, and anyway, I had a sense that I should be careful with him.

Maya and Jakob talked a little, the way people do. I pulled away from Jakob and began to sniff around the apartment. Not much had changed. My bed was gone, but my scent was still in the bedroom. It would be all right. I could sleep on the carpet or even on Jakob's bed, if he wanted me to.

I trotted back out to be with Jakob, passing Maya on the way. She reached out her hand, with its smell of soap and sweet lotion and tasty food, to stroke my back as I went by.

That's when it hit me – going back to Jakob would mean leaving Maya.

When Jakob had taken me away from my mother and my littermates, I hadn't had a choice. When Maya had taken me from the kennel to her home, I hadn't had a choice. I understood how it was. Dogs did not get to choose where they lived. People decided that.

But that didn't stop me from feeling like something inside me was tearing in two.

Jakob was far better at Work than Maya. But Maya didn't carry a dark core of sadness around with her all the time, the way that Jakob did. When Maya laughed, she was truly happy. When Maya hugged her little cousins and nieces and nephews at Mama's house, joy rippled off of her in waves. And when Maya petted me and scratched behind my ears and called me a good dog, I felt the same kind of love from her that I used to feel from Georgia. It was something Jakob never allowed himself to feel.

On the other hand, Jakob didn't have any cats . . .

I knew what I should do with my life – I had to Find, Show, and save people. I had once done that with Jakob. Now I did it with Maya, too. But what was happening now? Would I stay here with Jakob? Would I go home with Maya? Who would I do my Work with?

I began to pace anxiously, back and forth.

'Do you need to go out?' Maya asked.

'No. When she needs to do that, she sits by the door,' Jakob said.

'Oh. Right. I've seen her do that,' Maya said. 'I just leave my back door open a lot of the time, so, you know. She can come and go.'

They were silent for a little while. I didn't feel like sitting still, even near Jakob. I moved into the kitchen. It wasn't like Mama's kitchen; the floor was perfectly clean, as it always was. Nothing tasty to be licked up. Too bad. It would have made me feel better.

'I heard you're taking Disability,' Maya said.

'Yeah, well, I've been shot twice in the last five years; that'd be enough for anybody,' Jakob replied.

'You'll be missed,' Maya said quietly.

'I'm not leaving town. I'm enrolled at UCLA. Full-time. I only have a year and a half left for my law degree.'

There was another silence. Maya was uncomfortable; I could tell. It used to happen a lot around Jakob, when people would try to talk with him. The words would get slower and slower and then stop, and the other person would sit there quietly, getting more and more anxious.

I came back into the living room and wandered around in a circle, restless. Jakob was staring at me. 'So when are you up for certification?' he asked, as if he'd just noticed how quiet things had got.

I picked a spot on the floor halfway between the two of them and lay down with a sigh. I couldn't figure out what these two humans were going to do. I couldn't even figure out why they wanted to sit there and make words at each other if it wasn't going to make either one of them happy.

I wasn't happy, either.

'Two weeks, but . . .' Maya's voice trailed off.

'But?' Jakob prompted her.

'I'm thinking of resigning from the programme.' Maya's words came out in a rush, as if she was afraid she'd stop talking if she let herself slow down. 'I just can't keep up. I didn't realize . . . Well, someone else would probably be better.'

'You can't do that,' Jakob said sharply.

I raised my head and looked at him, wondering why he was angry.

'You can't keep switching handlers on a dog,' Jakob continued. 'Ellie is the best dog anybody's ever seen.'

I thumped my tail when I heard my name, but Jakob's tone was still stern.

'You dump her like that, you could ruin her,' he told Maya. 'Wally said the two of you have a real connection. I can see it, too. She's bonded with you. She looks to you. You're a team.'

'I'm just not cut out for it physically, Jakob.' Maya's voice had tears in it, but anger, too. I looked over a little anxiously at her. If they were both angry, I didn't know who I should go to first. Should I comfort Maya? Should I move closer to Jakob and calm him down?

Maybe I had missed something in the kitchen. I could go back in there . . .

'I'm not an ex-Marine like you,' Maya told Jakob. 'I'm just a beat cop who can barely pass the physical every year. I've been trying, but it is just too hard.'

'Too hard.' Jakob glared at her until Maya shrugged and looked away. Her anger dissolved into shame.

Jakob was still angry, but Maya was sad. That helped me decide what to do. I heaved myself up and went over to her, nuzzling her hand.

'What about how hard it would be on Ellie?' Jakob asked. 'Doesn't that matter?'

'Of course it matters.'

'You're saying you're not willing to work.'

I could sense the hot tears inside Maya and how hard she was fighting them back. I shoved my nose under her hand again. She felt better when she petted me; I knew she did. I felt better, too.

Maya smiled, even though the smile was wobbly at the corners. She ran her hand through the fur on my head. 'Oh, Ellie.'

She looked up at Jakob. 'Of course Ellie matters to

me, Jakob! How can you even say that? It's her I'm thinking of. She deserves a handler who can keep up with her. I'm saying I'm not cut out for this. I don't have what it takes inside.'

'What it takes. Inside.'

When Jakob spoke again, he wasn't looking at Maya and his voice was quieter.

'When I was shot the first time, my shoulder was so messed up, I had to learn to use it all over again. I went to physical therapy every day, and there was this little two-pound weight on a pulley, and that thing *hurt* . . . and my wife was in her final round of chemo. More than once, I wanted to give up. It was too *hard*.' Jakob turned his head and blinked at Maya. 'But Susan was dying. And she never gave up, not until the very end. And if she could keep going, I knew I had to. Because it's important. Because failure isn't an option if success is just a matter of more effort.'

The same old dark pain swirled around inside Jakob like a storm, and the anger inside him was gone, as if blown away by a gust of wind. I left Maya's side and went over to him, sitting at his feet, looking up into his face.

'I know it's difficult, Maya,' he said, and his voice was rough. 'Try harder.'

Jakob sagged in his chair, as if he was too tired to speak another word. And somehow I knew then that I

106

wouldn't be staying with Jakob. He just wasn't interested in Find any more.

Sadness was flowing through Maya, too, but she didn't seem tired, the way Jakob did. She sat up straighter. She looked stronger. I remembered the strength in her that day she took me running by the ocean, how she went further than she thought she ever could.

'OK. You're right,' she told Jakob.

Jakob came to the door with both of us and petted my head when we left. 'Goodbye, Maya. Goodbye, Ellie. You're a good girl,' he told me.

I licked his hand and smelt him one last time – the scent of his skin, his sweat, the dark pain that was inside him and the strength that was in him, too. Then I walked out of the building with Maya.

Jakob and Maya had decided my fate between them, and I was content. I was going to Work, and I was going to do it with Maya.

We were going to do it together.

A little while after we'd left Jakob's apartment, Maya took me running up in the hills. We ran together; I kept my pace slow so that she could keep up. After a while, I heard her gasp, and then a thump as she fell.

I came back quickly and put my nose in her face, smelling the salt of her sweat. Her knees were bleeding, and I smelt the salt there, too, and the stinging pain.

'OK, Ellie,' Maya said quietly, and pushed herself up

again. 'OK. Let's keep going.'

After that, we ran every day once we were finished with Work. It was gloriously fun. There were so many things to smell, and since we weren't Working, I could stop and sniff the traces left by other dogs, trails from rabbits and squirrels and cats, scraps of food in the grass, fascinating bits of rubbish. Sometimes Maya even pulled ahead of me and I'd dash after her to keep up.

I loved it. The only part I didn't love was how full of pain Maya was when we'd finally get back to the car. One night a few evenings after we'd been to see Jakob, she pulled into the driveway and simply sat there.

I got up, balanced on the back seat, ready to jump out. It was dinnertime. I was more than ready for something to eat.

But Maya didn't move.

I stuck my head into the front seat, near her face, to investigate. She put a hand forward to turn the key and make the car stop its annoying noise. But after that, she just sat still, sweat running down her face.

I could tell she was tired – too tired to get out of the car.

'I'm going to fail, Ellie,' she said softly, not turning around to look at me. 'I'm so sorry.'

I heard my name, but I couldn't tell what she wanted me to do. So I just waited as patiently as I could. I could see Emmet and Stella both watching from the window.

They probably didn't even know what a car was. They certainly never got to go running. But that was the way it should be. Dogs are superior animals. I know Maya liked her cats for some reason, but even she would have had to admit they were useless.

I couldn't even see Tinkerbell. Probably she'd heard the sound of the car and was cowering under something.

'Are you OK, Maya?'

It was a soft voice, and it was Al's. The wind had been blowing away from me, so I hadn't smelt him coming. I put my head out the window so that he could scratch my ears.

'Oh, hi, Al.' Maya seemed to wake up. She got out of the car, moving a little awkwardly, as if her legs were hurting her. 'Yes, I was just . . . thinking.'

'Oh. I saw you pull up in your car.'

'Yes.'

'So I came over to see if you needed any help.'

There it was again, Al's favourite word. I turned my head so that he could scratch behind my other ear.

'No, no. I was just running with the dog.'

Al opened the door for me, and I jumped out. I stared pointedly at Emmet and Stella, so that they would notice I was outside and they were in. They looked away in disgust.

'OK.' Al took a deep breath. 'You've lost weight, Maya.'

'What?' Maya stared at him.

Al seemed to shrink a little. 'Not that you were fat. I just noticed, in your shorts, your legs look so thin.' A gust of misery flowed off him, as if he'd been drenched in it, and he started to back away. 'I should go,' he said. I was sorry to see him leave. It meant no more ear scratching for a while. On the other hand, if he went away Maya would probably go inside and then we could have some dinner.

'Thank you, Al. That was sweet,' Maya said.

He stopped backing up and stood a little straighter. I could smell his relief. 'In my opinion, you don't need to exercise any more,' he said softly. 'You are perfect the way you are.'

Maya laughed. Al laughed. I wagged my tail to show the cats inside on the windowsill that I understood the joke and they didn't.

13

A week or so later, Maya and I went to Work. There were other dogs around, too, and people standing and watching. That wasn't what it was usually like, but I didn't mind. They couldn't distract me. I had a job to do.

When Maya told me to, I climbed up a tippy board, balanced while it moved, and carefully climbed down. She ordered me up on another board that was perched between two trestles, and I sat patiently until she said I could get down again.

Then Maya moved to one end of a long tube and called to me.

I remembered how I'd done this first for Jakob. I hadn't liked it then; the tube had seemed dark and frightening. Now it was easy, just part of Work. I plunged in, forcing my way through, to see Maya's face break into a wide smile when I wiggled out.

'Good girl, Ellie!'

Then she told me to Find.

This was my favourite part. The other commands were important to Maya, as they had been to Jakob. I understood that, and I didn't really mind climbing up unsteady boards or crawling into tubes. But Find was the most important. Find was what Work really meant.

I had my nose in the grass, sniffing eagerly. I caught a scent quickly: a man who smelt of peppermint gum, spicy cologne, coffee and a leather coat. Maya was nervous and excited; I could tell from her voice and the tension in her body. So I raced after the trail as quickly as I could, leaving her to follow behind.

In a patch of weeds I made my first Find: a pair of the man's socks. Humans were so odd about dropping their clothing. I wondered why they didn't just have fur; it would be much easier. I dashed back to Maya. She was breathing hard, but not gasping, when I found her. 'Show me!' she said quickly, after one look at my face.

She kept up with me, too, although she was starting to pant by the time we reached the socks. 'Good, Ellie. Good girl! Find!' she said again.

I dashed off, running through trees and bushes,

jumping over a muddy puddle, following the trail. This was easy. It was fun!

Then the scent seemed to lift off the ground. I paused with my nose up. The wind moved the man's smell towards me. It was stronger in the air now than it was on the ground, and I knew what that meant. Wally had pulled this trick on me more than once.

I looked up. There the man was, on a branch of a tree. He stayed very still, probably hoping I didn't know he was there. But he couldn't fool me!

I spun in my tracks and headed back to Maya. She was not far behind me. 'Show me!' she wheezed.

I did. She followed me, pushing through the bushes, ducking under branches. She grunted when a branch smacked her in the face, and I looked back. 'Show me!' she called again.

I sat down at the base of the tree, staring up. Maya jogged up next to me and paused, looking around in confusion.

'Ellie? He's not here. Why'd you stop, girl?'

I didn't move. My eyes were on the man. He was so still, he might have been just an extra branch in the tree.

'Ellie? Show me.'

I *was* showing her. I twitched in frustration, but I kept my gaze on the man. Jakob would have figured it out by now.

'Ellie? Ellie? Oh, good girl, Ellie!'

Maya looked up, and she grinned. The man swung down out of the tree. He was grinning, too.

Maya quickly pulled the rubber bone out of her pocket to play with me, and I felt her pride and happiness as we wrestled and tugged.

'You're quite a team,' said the man we'd found.

'Yes,' said Maya, and she let me have the bone, then went down on her knees to hug me around the neck. 'Yes, we are!'

That night Maya took me to Mama's house. It was packed with people. All the children were there, from the tall, lanky teenager Maya called Joe, to the little ones who were still more like puppies than people. Lots of adults, too. Everyone hugged Maya, and everyone kept petting me and saying my name.

'Now that you are certified, you need to eat,' Mama told Maya.

Then the doorbell rang. That didn't usually happen at Mama's house. People just burst in. I followed Mama to the door, and when she opened it she gasped with happiness and smiled even wider than she usually did.

It was Al. He had a bunch of flowers in his hand, which he gave to Mama. She gave him a kiss on the cheek and he blushed, but he was happy. He scratched my ears in that excellent way he had.

'I hear you're a good girl, Ellie,' he said, and I wagged.

The whole family got quiet when Al stepped out into the backyard. There were picnic tables set up with food all over them, and cans that had drinks inside them, and people were sitting and standing everywhere, with the young ones running and shouting. But they all stopped and turned their faces towards the doorway.

Then Maya went over to Al and he gently touched her cheek with his mouth. I felt nervousness from both of them, and I quickly dashed over in case there was something that needed to be done. Work, maybe, or a taco to eat? I was ready for anything.

Then Maya smiled widely and turned around, taking Al's hand. 'Al, this is my brother José and my sister Elisa. That little one there is Elisa's youngest, and this is . . .'

Maya kept talking. Nobody was nervous any more, so I wandered around the yard, eating tortilla chips and bits of hot dogs that the children snuck to me. Everybody seemed happy, and I couldn't tell if Al, or Maya, or Mama was the happiest of all.

After that party in Mama's backyard, Maya took me to the kennel at the police station on most days. I settled in with Cammie and Gypsy again, and when Maya took me out we Found all sorts of people. There were two children who'd wandered away from their house (I Found them beside a little stream, carefully collecting rocks and piling them up on the bank), and a woman who'd fallen off a horse and hurt her leg. Horses seemed about as useless as cats to me; I wondered why everyone just didn't have dogs instead.

The day we found the woman in the woods, Maya took me home in the car. But after she'd changed out of her uniform at home and put some food down for the cats, she called to me again and we walked across the street to Al's house.

I could tell that Al was nervous again as soon as he opened the door. 'Maya, you look . . . y-y-ou look fantastic,' he stammered.

Maya laughed. 'Oh, Al, I do not,' she said, as if she wasn't sure. 'You're just not used to seeing me out of uniform, that's all.'

'Um. Come on in?' Al backed up and let us come into the living room.

I was pleased to discover that there were no cats here. I quickly sniffed around the living room while Al brought Maya a glass of something cold to drink and they sat on the couches, sometimes talking and sometimes just sitting.

There was a funny smell coming from the kitchen. I quickly checked it out. There was all sorts of food scattered around the counter; I could smell bread, and lettuce, and tomatoes, and onions that made my nose sting. But something in the oven did not smell right. I shook my head so that my collar rang, trying to get the smell out of my nose, and backed away into the living room.

'Oh, Ellie, silly dog, what are you doing?' Maya said.

Al jumped up. 'The chicken!' he gasped, and ran into the kitchen. The smell was much worse when he opened the oven door.

Al and Maya ran around opening windows. Maya tried not to laugh until Al started to, and then they both laughed together so much Maya had to sit down at the table until she could breathe again. Then Al brought the food, including the funny-smelling chicken, out to the table where Maya was waiting.

'No, Al, it's good,' Maya said, chewing. 'Really it is. Can I have some more?'

Al stared at her and shook his head. Then he got up and walked over to a phone.

'Hello?' he said, loud enough so that Maya could hear clearly. 'Can I order a large pepperoni with extra cheese? . . . Half an hour? Sounds great.'

Then he sat down at the table again, and he and Maya laughed some more. Al put some pieces of the chicken on a plate and set them on the floor for me.

I sniffed them. They were dry and coated with some-thing black that tasted like smoke.

'See, Al, it's not so bad. Ellie likes it!' Maya said, giggling.

'I think she's only being polite. Like you.'

When the pizza came, Al gave me a piece of that, too. It tasted much better than the chicken.

14

One day Maya took me to the airport, a busy place full of strange smells – diesel fumes, tar, disinfectant on the floors, and many, many people. I had to ride in my crate in a dark, noisy room for a very long time. At last Maya appeared again to take me out and clip a leash on my collar.

She walked out with me to a stretch of tarmac, which felt hot on my feet. Helicopters were nearby, blades whirring. I remembered the day Jakob had been taken away on one of those, and I stuck close to Maya's side.

But the helicopter didn't take Maya away. She climbed in, but she called to me and I jumped in after her. I was back to being a chopper dog! It wasn't as much fun as a car ride; the loud noise hurt my ears. But I was glad about it, all the same. Being a chopper dog meant I got to stay with Maya, and it meant I was going somewhere to Work.

We landed in a place like nowhere I'd ever been.

There were lots of dogs and police officers hurrying past. Sirens wailed. The air was thick with smoke and dust. I didn't like the smells at all.

There was something wrong with the buildings. Their walls were tilted; their doors hung lopsidedly or had been wrenched off. Roofs had holes in them or had slid off the buildings entirely and lay in heaps of boards and shingles on the ground.

Maya didn't seem sure where to go after we'd got off the helicopter. She stood still on the slab of tarmac where we had landed, looking around. 'Oh, Ellie,' she said, very softly, just for me to hear.

I pressed against her leg, feeling the fear in the tension of her muscles. It made me nervous; the strange smells and noises did, too. I yawned anxiously, wishing we could start Work. I wouldn't feel nervous when I was Working.

A man came up to us. His clothes and his skin were smeared with dirt and oil; his hair was hidden under a plastic helmet. He held out a hand to Maya and one to me. It smelt of ashes, blood and clay.

'I'm coordinating the US response in this sector,' he told Maya. 'Thanks for coming down.'

'I had no idea it was going to be this bad,' Maya said. Her voice shook the tiniest bit.

'Oh, this is just the tip of the iceberg. The El Salvadoran government is completely overwhelmed,' the man said. 'We've got more than four thousand people injured, hundreds dead. And we're still finding folks trapped. There've been more than half a dozen aftershocks since the earthquake on thirteenth January, some of them pretty bad. Be careful going into these places.'

Maya put me on a leash and led me out into the streets.

We had to climb over piles of stones and concrete blocks or find a way around piles of splintered boards with nails sticking out of them. Everything was coated with dust and ash. Soon it was all over Maya's hair and clothes, all over my fur, sticking to my nose. I didn't like it at all.

We came to a house with a crack along one side that reached from the foundation to the roof. 'Don't go in,' a man said, rubbing sweat out of his eyes. 'That roof won't be up for much longer.'

'Ellie, find!' Maya said. But she kept the leash on my collar and called me back when I tried to go in the open door. We just checked along the outside of the house. I smelt mostly dust and ashes, dirt underneath. Smoke in the air. No people.

If sadness had a smell, this would be it.

We checked other houses. Sometimes Maya let me inside, sometimes not. I didn't Find anyone in the first two.

Alongside the third house, I Found my first person.

One wall had tumbled, and the roof had crashed down as if it were made of paper. I smelt something at once and pulled quickly at the leash. Maya followed, kicking aside boards and shingles and glass, as I dragged her towards the ruined wall.

The person I'd Found smelt . . . wrong. I could smell a woman, smell her hair and the shampoo she'd used. But I also smelt blood and something else. Something cold and still.

I stopped, my attention focused on a pile of concrete blocks.

'There, Ellie? Somebody's there?' Maya asked.

I didn't move.

'Here!' she called.

Men came with shovels and crowbars, pulling aside the broken concrete blocks. I sat watching tensely. I'd Found somebody, but it didn't feel right. Wally had never hidden under something as big and heavy as this pile of crushed and cracked stone, so I wasn't sure what would happen next. Maybe when they got all the concrete blocks moved and I could see who I'd Found everything would feel all right.

Maya knelt down beside me. 'Good girl, Ellie,' she

whispered. But her 'good girl' felt wrong, too. She wasn't excited and happy. She was crying.

'OK,' one of the men said. 'We got her.'

'It's a woman?' Maya asked, wiping away tears and getting to her feet. 'She's . . .'

'Yeah. Too late. We'll get her out, but you can move on.'

I stared up at Maya, looking over at the men, who kept on digging, and then returning my gaze to Maya's face.

'Good girl, Ellie.' Maya straightened her back and pulled my old rubber bone out of her pocket. 'You did your job. Good girl!'

She played tug-of-war with me, but it wasn't like it usually was. I was anxious to keep Working. Maybe next time it would be better.

It wasn't. I Found three more people. They all had that same cold, dull smell. None of them moved. No one was happy that I'd Found them.

This wasn't right. Finding people was about saving them. I knew that these people could not be saved.

When Maya held the bone in front of me for the fourth time, I turned my head away.

'Oh, Ellie.' Tears ran down her face, making marks in the pale dust on her cheeks. 'It's not your fault, Ellie. You're a good girl.'

Her words didn't help. I felt like a bad dog. I was doing Find wrong. I was not saving anyone.

I lay down in the dirt and gritty rubble at Maya's feet. For the first time since Jakob had started showing me how to Work, I didn't want to do it any more. I wished we could go home. I wouldn't even mind Stella lying in my bed or Emmet sniffing at my food.

'Vernon?' Maya called to one of the men with shovels. 'Would you do me a favour and go and hide somewhere?'

'Hide?' He stared at her blankly.

'She needs to find someone alive. Would you go and hide? Like over in that house we just searched. And when she locates you, act all excited.'

'Um, yeah, OK.'

Without much interest, I watched Vernon walk away. Maya knelt down and patted me, then poured a little water from a bottle into my mouth. I lapped it up and she scratched my ears.

'OK, Ellie, ready? Ready to Find?'

I got up slowly. I was tired. And I could tell Maya was not as excited as she was pretending to be. But it was Work, so I followed her directions. She took me over to a house we'd already searched.

Why were we going back here? I paused in the doorway, puzzled, while Maya waited in the street. Something was different. I put my nose down to the dusty carpet and sniffed.

Vernon. His smell had been in here before, of course, but now it was fresher. And he'd walked straight across

124

the floor. I followed, stepping over bits of glass, books that had fallen from a bookcase, a toy truck, a smashed radio.

There was a pile of blankets in the corner. Vernon's smell was strong there, full of sweat and heat and goats. He smelt different from the other people I'd Found so far in this place. He smelt . . . alive.

I turned and raced back to Maya. 'Show me!' she urged.

I ran back to the blankets, and when Maya peeled them back Vernon sat up. A big smile crossed his sad, grubby face.

'You found me! Good dog, Ellie!' he shouted. I wagged so hard that my back feet started dancing with excitement. I was a good dog after all! I'd Found somebody who was glad to be Found!

Vernon laughed at my dance and rolled with me in the blankets. I licked his face. He tasted sweaty and dusty. Maya threw him the rubber bone, and we played tug-of-war.

Then I was ready to Work some more.

Maya and I Worked all night. We Found more people, including Vernon, who became better and better at hiding. But I'd worked with Wally, so no one could fool me for very long. I found Vernon every time.

The sun was coming up when we came to a new building. Sharp-smelling smoke was still rising in slow clouds from one corner. There was a smell here that I did not like at all. Some metal barrels had been crushed under chunks of concrete and were leaking a liquid that made my eyes water. It didn't smell like anything I'd ever smelt before.

Maya kept the leash on my collar. 'Careful, Ellie,' she murmured.

A brick wall had fallen down. I pushed away the horrible smell from the barrels, trying to Find. The smell was faint underneath the chemical stink, but I still caught it. A person. Dead.

I stopped and stared at the pile of bricks. 'Someone's here!' Maya called out. Her voice was tired.

'We know about him,' a man with a shovel told Maya. 'We can't get him out yet. Whatever's in those barrels is toxic. Going to need a clean-up crew.'

'OK, good dog. Let's go somewhere else, Ellie.'

I got up, but I didn't walk away with Maya. There was something, a hint of a new smell underneath the flood of chemical odours. There! The scent trickled out from a wide crack in the wall just beyond the pile of bricks. Another person. A woman.

My body went rigid. I looked up at Maya, waiting for 'Show me!'

'It's OK, Ellie. We're going to leave this one here. Come on,' Maya said. She pulled gently at my leash again. 'Come, Ellie.'

I stared back at the crack in the wall, then up at Maya. We couldn't leave!

This new person I had found smelt like Vernon. She smelt alive.

15

'We see the victim, Ellie. We're going to have to leave him here. Come on,' Maya said.

She wanted me to leave. But why? We weren't done. We hadn't Found the person I had smelt.

Unless . . .

Was Maya confused? Did she think I was still telling her about the person under the bricks? That wasn't right. I stared up at her, trying to tell her with my eyes, my ears, my tense and rigid body, that I had Found someone new.

I needed Maya to understand. I could not Find without her. Finding meant bringing Maya to a person. What would I do if she wouldn't come?

'Does she want to Find me again?' Vernon asked.

Maya shook her head. 'Poor Ellie. This is so confusing for her. You can't hide around here; it's too dangerous. Tell you what, though, it would be fun for her to chase you a little. Go up the street a bit and call her, and I'll let her off the leash.'

I didn't pay attention to Vernon as he trotted away. I was still on Find. My focus was on the rubble, on the crack with the faint smell drifting out of it.

The person was alive and frightened. I could smell fear, sharp beneath the chemical smell that hurt my nose.

Maya unsnapped my leash. 'Ellie? What's Vernon doing? Where's he going?'

'Hey, Ellie! Look!' Vernon shouted. He started to run slowly up the street, glancing back over his shoulder at me.

I stared after him. It would be fun to chase him. Maya wanted me to, and I liked Finding Vernon. He'd wrestle and play with me, and he was glad to be Found. Finding him had been the only fun part of this night.

But I had Work to do. I turned back to the collapsed building.

'Ellie! No!' Maya called.

If it had been Jakob, that 'no!' would have stopped me in my tracks. But Maya just didn't command me with the same force. She was more frightened than angry. It showed in her voice.

I scrambled over the pile of bricks that lay over the dead body, scrabbling my way forward. My feet slipped in something wet, and the pads started to sting. That harsh, unnatural smell was rising all around me. It was blocking out the woman's scent. I clawed my way forward, trying to find it again.

There! The crack in the wall was ahead. I pushed my way into it. I'd done this before, wriggling through the tube. First with Jakob, then with Maya. I knew what to do.

Something wet and slick was underneath me. It was sticking to my fur. It splashed up on to my nose as I forced my way forward. It hurt! My nose stung even worse than my paws. I pushed myself forward faster, desperate to get out of this cramped, dark, dangerous place.

Then the ground vanished beneath me. I'd dropped down into a narrow shaft. I hit the concrete floor hard and staggered back up, shaking my head hard. My nose! It was burning!

I couldn't even smell the woman huddled in a corner of the shaft, pressing a piece of cloth that she'd torn off her skirt to her face. Her eyes were wide and dark as she looked at me, shocked.

I couldn't get back to Maya to Show her what I'd Found. I barked instead.

'Ellie!' Maya's voice echoed off the concrete walls around me, and she started to cough.

'Get back, Maya,' Vernon warned.

I kept barking. 'Ellie!' Maya shouted again, sounding closer.

The woman heard Maya. The cloth dropped away from her face, and she started screaming, all of her terror and pain tumbling out of her in her voice.

'Here! I'm here! Don't leave me in here! Get me out!'

'There's someone in there, someone alive!' Maya shouted.

I could tell Maya understood, at last. So I stopped barking and went to sit down beside the woman I'd Found. I kept shaking my head and pawing at my nose with my paw. My eyes were watering, and whatever had got on my nose was getting worse and worse.

The woman saw. Gently she tried to pat at my nose with the piece of cloth she'd held over her face.

I jerked away and growled. I couldn't help it. Her touch had made the stinging flare into sharp, angry pain.

I felt bad for growling. I knew that wasn't what I was supposed to do. So I crept back to her side and licked her hand to apologize. She seemed to understand and didn't try to touch my nose again. Instead she whispered quietly to herself, words that were quiet and urgent at once.

I'd heard Mama talk like that once. She'd called it praying.

The woman and I sat together until a man wearing a helmet and a mask poked a torch into the space and waved it around. The light fell on both of us, and the woman gasped and then waved frantically.

Soon the sounds of digging and hammering drifted down, and then a square of daylight broke into the shaft from above. A shadow blocked it almost at once. A man was swinging down on a rope.

The woman had obviously never practised being lifted by a rope harness before. She was very frightened and kept praying the whole time while the fireman buckled the straps around her and hoisted her out. But Jakob had taught me that a harness was not to be feared, so I stepped calmly in when it was my turn.

I went up in jerks and stops to the top of the shaft. Maya was there when they hauled me through the hole the men had dug. I jumped into her arms as soon as they unclipped the harness from my back.

Maya's relief turned quickly to alarm. 'Oh no, Ellie. Your nose!'

Maya clipped on my leash and ran with me quickly to a fire truck. Maya talked to one of the firefighters, her voice urgent. He came over to me and then – well, as if things weren't bad enough, he actually gave me a bath!

A bath! Weren't we Working? I was disgusted, but I sat still when Maya told me to. Actually, it was more of a rinsing than a bath. The firefighter held up a hose and sluiced cool water over my face and fur. At first it made my nose sting worse and I jerked away, but soon the tender skin felt a little better.

Work was over after that. Maya took me back for another helicopter ride and then on an aeroplane. Once we were back at the airport, she put me in her car and drove me straight to a man in a cool white room.

He wore a white coat and smelt of other dogs and of harsh soap and disinfectant. I'd been here before. The man's voice was kind and his hands were gentle, but often there were injections involved, so he wasn't my favourite person.

He held my face in his hands and looked at me carefully. Then he took a tube out of a jar and rubbed some kind of cream gently into my nose. The cream smelt awful, but it felt cool and wonderful, so I let him do it without protesting.

'What was it, some kind of acid?' he asked Maya.

'I don't know. Is she going to be OK?' Maya's hand was on my neck, rubbing the fur gently. I felt her love and concern in her touch and her voice, and I wished I could let her know I was feeling better. My nose didn't hurt as much as before, and the cream had taken the last of the stinging away.

'We'll want to watch out for any signs of infection,' the man in the white coat told Maya, 'but I don't see any reason why she shouldn't heal up just fine.'

'But will she be able to work?' Maya's voice was still worried.

The man shook his head. 'We'll have to wait and see.'

Maya and I didn't do any Work for the next two weeks or so. Every day, she gently rubbed the cream into my nose. Emmet and Stella seemed to find this pretty amusing and would sit on the counter and watch. It was embarrassing, letting the cats stare at me like that, but Maya told me to hold still, so I did.

Tinkerbell, though . . . she *loved* that cream. I can't imagine why, but cats are strange and that's all there is to it. After Maya had finished with me, the little grey-and-white cat would come out of wherever she'd been hiding and sniff at my nose for a long time. Then she'd rub against me and purr.

This was even more embarrassing than the cat audience on the counter. I'd lie down with a sigh, and Tinkerbell would sit and smell me, her tiny nose bobbing up and down. She even started curling up against me to sleep.

It was almost more than I could stand. I couldn't wait for Maya to tell me it was time to go back to Work.

At last, she did. When we got to the park, I bounded up to Wally and Belinda. They were excited, too. I could see it in their wide grins and hear it in their voices.

'I hear you are the hero dog, Ellie! Good dog!' I wagged even harder when Wally praised me. Praise was nice. Petting was good. But best of all, we were about to go to Work!

Wally ran off while Belinda and Maya sat down at a picnic table.

'So how are you and Wally doing?' Maya said.

I sat, but it was hard. My legs were twitching with eagerness to be up and running. If we went after him now, we could Find Wally right away.

'He's taking me to meet his parents over the Fourth, so . . .' Belinda replied.

'That's good.'

I groaned. Humans could do so many amazing things – why did they sit still and make words so often? They were not even interesting words, like 'Find' or 'Come' or 'walk' or 'good dog'.

'Down, Ellie,' Maya said. That was not an interesting word, either. I flopped down with a sigh, looking pointedly in the direction Wally had taken.

Maya and Belinda kept on making their uninteresting words. Finally, just when I was about to burst from impatience Maya looked up with a smile.

'OK, Ellie. You can't wait, huh, girl? Find!'

I took off. It was marvellous, being able to run, and Maya was able to keep up with me now. There was nothing better in the world than this.

Wally had got much better at hiding! It was strange. I couldn't find his scent at all. I checked the grass, and then I lifted my nose, searching for any trace of him. There weren't many other smells today to distract me, but I still couldn't find the familiar scent that was Wally.

I ran back and forth, checking the grass and the air, turning my head into every breeze. Nothing.

I dashed back to Maya, to make sure we were still Working. 'Find, Ellie,' she said again. I could hear a little worry in her voice, but she didn't need to worry. I was good at Work. I liked Find. Wally was just being extra clever this time, but he could not fool me for long.

Maya let me Work for a while, and then she called me. We moved to a new area of the park and I tried again. Grass, nothing. Bushes, nothing. Wind, nothing. No Wally anywhere.

'What's the matter, girl? You OK?'

I snapped my head around, startled. It was Wally!

How could that have happened? How could Wally have snuck up on me? The wind was behind him, blowing from him to me. And yet I'd heard him before I smelt him. I rocketed towards him until, at last, my nose picked up on the smell I'd been expecting. Then I dashed back to Maya. I didn't need to Show her where Wally was this time, though. She was already talking to him.

'We're having sort of an off day!' she called out as he came towards us.

'I guess so. I've never seen her fail before. Hey, Ellie, how are you doing?' Wally asked me. He held out a stick to me and we played a little, tugging each other across the grass.

'Tell you what, Maya. You focus her attention away from me. I'm going to go over that ridge, there, and double back a little. Give me about ten minutes,' said Wally.

'You sure?'

'She's been out of action for a couple of weeks; let's give her an easy one.'

I may not have seen Wally leaving, but I heard him, even though Maya had offered me the rubber bone and was now (in that way humans had) trying to get it back from me. I could hear him and I knew he was hiding again. I wrestled happily with the bone, shaking my head to tear it loose from Maya's grip. We were going to Find again!

'OK, Ellie!' Maya pulled the bone loose from my teeth. 'Find!'

I took off eagerly, heading in the direction I'd heard

Wally go. I ran up a small hill and stopped, not sure what to do next.

How was Wally doing it? How was he hiding his scent? Not even the breeze was bringing me a hint of it.

I ran back to Maya for direction. She sent me off to my right. I snaked back and forth, searching.

No Wally.

Maya sent me left. Again, no sign of Wally. I dashed back to Maya and stared up at her face eagerly, excited but a little anxious, too. Was there a clue? Something I was missing? Would she tell me? We had to Find him!

Maya sent me left again and followed me this time. She walked with me around the base of the hill I'd climbed earlier. I searched in grass and scrubby bushes, lifting my nose to the wind. But Wally had been very clever. I had no idea where he was.

Then something moved.

It was just a ripple in the grass, but it caught my eye. I jumped, focused on the place. Wally sat up. I'd done it! I'd Found him! But there was no need to run back to Maya; she was already standing there.

'This isn't good, is it?' Maya asked. 'The vet said she should be fully recovered by now.'

'Well . . . let's give it another week, see if she gets any better,' Wally said. He felt sad, for some reason, so I nuzzled his hand. He was usually very happy to be Found. I didn't know why this time it was different.

Maya and I Worked a few more times after that, but Wally kept on fooling me, somehow. He'd disguise his scent so that I couldn't pick it up until I was nearly standing on him.

Then Maya and I stopped going to the park at all.

16

'What does it mean that Ellie is decertified? Does it mean you will lose your job?' Al asked one night. I'm not a big fan of feet, but I'd allowed Al to take off his shoes and rub my tummy with his because they didn't smell as bad as usual.

'No, but I'll be reassigned. I've been on a desk for the past several weeks, but I'm not really cut out for that. I'll probably request a transfer to go back out on patrol,' Maya answered.

Without letting Maya see, Al dropped a tiny piece of meat on the carpet in front of me. It was one of the main reasons I liked to lie in front of him at meals, even if it meant I had to put up with his feet. I silently licked up the treat while Stella gave me a dirty look from the couch.

'I don't like to think of you being out on patrol,' Al told Maya. 'It is so dangerous.'

'Albert.' Maya sighed.

'What about Ellie?'

I looked up at my name. More treats? No. Al didn't hand down any more meat.

'I don't know. She can't work any more; her sense of smell is too damaged. So she'll be retired. She'll live with me. Right, Ellie?'

I wagged. I always liked the way Maya said my name, even if she didn't drop down anything from her plate. You could hear how much she loved me in the simple sound.

'Let's go to the beach,' Al suggested. 'No, leave the dishes for later. Come on, while it's still light.'

'Let's bring Ellie.'

'Of course, let's bring Ellie.'

Al had brought a blanket to the beach, and he spread it out on the sand. The sun was going down, and the breeze took on a chill. He wrapped an arm around Maya's shoulders and they talked while the little waves came in.

'It's so beautiful,' Maya said.

I figured they probably wanted to play with a stick or a ball or something, but she had my leash on so that I couldn't go and Find them anything. It was too bad. They had nothing to do.

Al got my attention by becoming afraid. His heart started to pound so loudly I could hear it, and I could smell the sweat that broke out on his palms and his forehead. I could sense the nervous tension that was tightening all his muscles.

I looked around anxiously. What was going to happen? I moved a little closer to Maya, ready to save her if she needed it.

'Maya, when you m-m-moved here . . .' Al stammered. 'So many months I wanted to talk to you. You are so beautiful.'

Maya laughed. 'Oh, Al, I'm not beautiful; come on.'

Some boys ran down by the water, tossing a thin plastic saucer through the air. I watched it alertly, in case it turned out to be the thing Al was so nervous about. It didn't look dangerous; it looked like it would be fun to chase, actually.

'You are the most wonderful woman in the world,' Al said. 'I . . . I love you, Maya.'

Maya was starting to feel afraid, too. I nudged my nose under her hand, in case she needed comforting. She always petted me when I did that. But this time she didn't.

'I love you, too, Al.'

'I know I'm not rich. I know I'm not handsome . . .' Al said.

'Oh my . . .' Maya breathed. Her heart was beating fast now, too.

'But I will love you all my life, if you will let me.' Al turned on the blanket, rising on his knees. 'Will you marry me, Maya?'

It wasn't too long after that day that Maya and Mama and all of the people we saw so often at Mama's house came together in a big white building and sat quietly to watch me do a new trick Maya had taught me. I walked very slowly down a narrow path between long wooden benches, climbed up some carpeted stairs, and stood patiently while Al took something out of a little pack that he'd already tied on my back.

Maya whispered, 'Good girl, Ellie!' She was wearing a big, fluffy dress, so I knew we weren't going to Work afterwards or to the park for a run. But I didn't mind, because everybody seemed so happy. Mama was even sniffing back tears of joy. I must have done the trick really well, I thought, sitting down to wait while Maya and Al and another man in a dark suit talked and talked and talked.

Then we went to Mama's house and the children ran around and fed me cake.

Soon after that, Maya and Al did something strange. They took everything in Maya's house and stuffed it all into big boxes. Then they did the same with all of Al's things. I didn't understand why they needed so many things anyway; I was content with just my dog bed and my food dish. Maybe they'd decided that was all they needed, too.

But it didn't turn out that way.

'Come, Ellie!' Maya called the day after all the boxes had been carried into a big truck. 'Car ride!'

I still loved car rides, even though we never got to go to Work any more. I bounced into the back seat. But Maya did something I didn't understand at all; she came out of the house carrying two big cases, and then she went back for a third. When she put the cases in the back of the car, I heard angry and frightened meowing coming from inside. Stella, Emmet and Tinkerbell were in there!

Cats did not come on car rides! Car rides were only for dogs. I barked at Maya to let her know she'd made a mistake.

'Calm down, Ellie. Cool it, cats!' Maya said, getting into the car and shutting the door. 'It's a short ride. Don't worry. We'll be there soon.'

'There' turned out to be a new house.

I approved of the house. It had a much nicer back-yard than our old one. And there was a big bed, too, which Maya let Al share with her. That wasn't fair; she had never let me share!

So that first night I made a plan. After Maya and Al had been quiet for a while, I crept up to the bed and worked my nose under the quilt. Nobody stirred. My plan was working!

I wiggled up so that my front legs were under the covers, too. Then it was just a matter of jumping so my back legs could make it as well. I jumped.

'What's— Ellie!' Al shouted.

'Oh, Ellie!' Maya was groaning and laughing at the same time. 'Oh, Al, I'm sorry. She never did that before.'

'Oh, whatever. Let her stay.' Al reached down and scratched my ears. 'But on *top* of the quilt, Ellie! Not under the blankets!'

At last! I curled up at Maya's feet and she tucked her toes under me to keep them warm.

But after a few nights, I decided that sleeping on the big bed was not as much fun as it had seemed. There wasn't that much room, and the cats didn't get the message that they belonged on the floor now that I was allowed on the bed with Maya and Al.

I jumped down and decided that I'd much rather sleep on the fuzzy rug on Maya's side of the bed. That way I was able to get up and follow her if she woke up in the middle of the night and wanted a glass of water or went to read a book in the living room.

Maya still took me for car rides. Sometimes we went to the beach to run, and Al came with us now and then, but he had trouble keeping up. Maya and I went to the park for long walks, too. But I began to understand that we were not going to do Work again.

We must have Found all the people who needed to be Found. And maybe Wally and Belinda just didn't want to play any more. I didn't really understand it. I missed Find, and I missed the sense that Maya and I were doing something important together. That we were a team, the way Jakob and I had been.

But if Maya didn't want to Work any more, I guessed we would not be doing it.

So I was surprised the day that Maya, dressed in her uniform, called to me. 'Ready for work, Ellie?' she asked.

My ears perked up. *Work? Really?*

I nearly knocked her over, dashing to the car.

One thing puzzled me. Maya was relaxed, not tense. She was smiling, not serious. She had never been like this before when we were going to Work. I wondered why.

She pulled the car up in front of a big building and took me up to the front door.

'It's a school, Ellie. You're going to like it here. Lots of kids, just like at Mama's house.'

Maya opened the big doors and we went inside.

There were lots of kids in the building, many more than at Mama's house! Maya took me into a big, noisy room with a stage up front and rows and rows of children sitting in chairs. They started laughing and calling out as soon as they caught sight of me.

'Dog! Look at the dog!'

'Can I pet her?'

'She's so *cute*!'

Maya and I walked up some stairs to the stage. She told me to Sit, and I did it. Someone must have told the children to Sit as well, but they were not very good at it yet. They wiggled and bounced and got up on their knees to see better.

A woman got up and talked to the children. I wasn't paying much attention to her voice, since I didn't know it well. 'Use your listening ears,' I heard her say, and 'best manners, please' and 'a real welcome'. Then all the children clapped. The noise startled me, and they laughed.

I wagged. The joy that I could see in their faces and hear in their giggling voices made me happy, even though there didn't seem to be much to do here.

Maya walked me forward, and when she spoke her voice was loud.

'This is Ellie.' I perked up my ears, looking up to see if a command would follow. 'She is a retired search-and-rescue dog. As part of our outreach programme, I wanted to come to talk to you about how Ellie has helped find lost children, and what you can do if you ever become lost,' Maya said.

No command. I sat down and yawned.

I waited for about half an hour while Maya talked. Then she led me down off the stage. The children lined up and came in small groups to pet me. Some gave me grabby hugs; some hung back, a little afraid. One girl timidly offered me her hand, and I licked it, tasting salty crackers and a smudge of chocolate. She jumped back with a squeal, but she was giggling.

After that, Maya and I did School often. Sometimes the children were younger, sometimes older. The younger ones gave me more hugs. The older ones scratched behind my ears. Either one was fine with me.

Sometimes we went to other buildings, where there were no children at all but people as old as Marilyn, one of the first people I'd ever Found. Or to places that had sharp, chemical smells. I couldn't smell as much any more, but those places reminded me of the liquid that had splashed on to my nose and hurt it. I didn't like the smell, but I did like the people. They were lying in beds or sitting in strange chairs with wheels, and I could smell and feel that they were sad, or sick, or in pain. But some of that sadness lifted when Maya talked to them and they stroked my fur.

I wasn't saving these people, exactly. They weren't lost – except that it sort of felt as if they were. Somehow, this was a new kind of Work. I didn't really understand it, but Maya was there and people were happier when we left. That seemed right. That was what Work was for: to make things better.

17

When we weren't doing School or our other Work, Maya would run out the door in the morning in a big hurry while Al chuckled. Then Al would leave, too. I'd stay at home with the stupid cats.

Even though I no longer wore the nose cream, Tinkerbell didn't leave me alone. She curled up against me when I took my naps on the soft blanket Maya had put down near her bed. It was embarrassing, really, but since no one except Emmet and Stella was there to see, I let Tinkerbell stay. The feel of her purr vibrated against my side. It was a warm feeling, somehow, and it reminded me a little of snuggling close with Mother and my brothers and sisters, long ago.

One day Maya called to me and I jumped into the car, ready to Work. 'Look at those clouds, Ellie,' she said as she drove.

I wagged, happy just to hear her talking to me, and stuck my nose out of the car window. The air was damp and sweet. I loved mornings like this. The smells were stronger than usual, more like I remembered them from the old days, when we still did Find. I smelt tar, exhaust fumes, salty French fries from a store that we drove past, other dogs, people.

When Maya pulled the car up in front of a school, she ran inside quickly with me as the first drops of rain started to fall.

This time, we didn't go to one of the big rooms where the children sat in seats and Maya's voice boomed. Instead, we walked into a smaller place called a classroom. The children sat on blankets on the floor. That looked cosy. If they wanted me to lie down on a blanket, too, I would not have minded.

While I was waiting to see if someone would offer me a blanket, I stretched out on the carpet.

Maya had just started talking when a sudden flash of brilliant light brightened all the windows. Then came a crack of thunder. Some of the children jumped and yelped like frightened puppies. The rain poured down. I lifted my nose and breathed deeply, wishing someone would open a window to let the smells inside.

'Settle down, class,' said a woman standing near Maya.

The door to the classroom swung open and a man, his jacket dripping wet, came inside. A woman was with him. I sat up quickly, looking straight at them.

'We've lost Geoffrey Hicks,' the man said.

I knew the worry in his voice, the tension in his muscles, the way alarm was rising off both of them, like a scent. This was the way people looked and sounded when I was about to Work.

'He's a first-grader,' the man told Maya.

'They were playing hide-and-seek when the rain started,' the woman said. 'The storm just came up out of nowhere. One minute it was fine, the next—' She put her hand up to her eyes, which were suddenly full of tears. 'When I got everyone to come in, Geoffrey wasn't with them. It was his turn to hide.'

'Could the dog . . .' the man said hesitantly, turning to Maya.

Maya looked at me, and I sat up straighter. Was this Work?

'You'd better call 911,' she said. 'Ellie hasn't worked a search or rescue in years.'

'Won't the rain wash away the scent? It's really coming down out there,' said the woman, fighting to keep her voice steady. 'I'm worried that by the time another dog gets here . . .'

Maya bit her lip. 'We'll certainly help look. You need to call the police, though. Where do you think he might have gone?'

'There are some woods behind the playground,' the man said quickly. 'There's a fence, but the kids can lift it up. They know they're not supposed to, but sometimes . . .'

'This is his backpack; will that help?' the woman asked, holding out a canvas bag.

'Maybe.' Maya took it. 'Call the police! Ellie, Come!'

I jumped to my feet and raced after her as she ran down the hallway. At last! We were going to Find again!

Maya stopped just inside a door. Outside, rain was pounding down. 'Look at it rain,' she muttered. Her nervous energy sagged. She knelt down beside me, and I felt her worry and her sadness but her determination, too. 'Ellie, you ready, girl? Here, smell this.'

I took a deep whiff of the canvas bag. I could smell strawberry yogurt, cookie crumbs, paper, crayons and a person. 'Geoffrey, Geoffrey,' Maya said. 'OK?' She opened the door and the rain whipped into the hallway. 'Find!'

I leaped out into the rain. In front of me was a wide stretch of black pavement and beyond that a playground piled with wood chips. I coursed back and forth, my nose low to the ground. I could smell many children, although the smells were not strong and the rain was starting to wash them away.

Maya was out, running away from the school. 'Here, Ellie! Find here!' she shouted over the drumming of the raindrops on the hard ground.

We tracked all the way back to a wire fence. Nothing. I could feel Maya's frustration and fear, and it made me tense inside. Was I doing this wrong? Was I being a bad dog?

Maya found a piece of the fence, next to a pole, that had been bent back to make a triangle-shaped hole. 'Find, Ellie!' she commanded. I sniffed all along the fence, but I could Find nothing. 'OK, if he'd gone through that, you'd smell him, right? I hope so,' she murmured. 'Geoffrey!' she shouted. 'Geoffrey, come on out! It's all right!'

No one came out.

'Keep trying,' Maya said softly. 'Find, Ellie!'

We followed the length of the fence all the way around the school yard. Nothing. A police car pulled up on the street outside the fence, red lights flashing through the rain. Maya jogged over to talk to the man driving.

I was still on Find. I kept going, my nose to the ground. It was hard. I wasn't picking up much of anything, and the rain was washing so much away. But I knew if I just concentrated I could separate the smell of the backpack, the smell that was Geoffrey, from all the others. Jakob had trained me. Maya had Worked with me. They'd shown me how to do it. I could still do it, if I just didn't quit—

There! I had something. I whipped my head around again and sniffed harder. Right in the middle of the fence, there was a gap between two poles. No grown person would be able to squeeze through, but Geoffrey had done it. His scent had been rubbed on both of the poles, strongly enough that the rain had not washed them clean.

Geoffrey had left the playground.

I dashed back to Maya. She was speaking to the policeman when I got to her feet. 'We tried, but it's no good. Ellie can't—'

Then Maya turned to look at me, shocked. 'Ellie?' she said. Her voice came out as a whisper. Then it got stronger. 'Ellie, Show me!'

We ran back through the rain to the two poles. Maya peered through the small gap. 'Come on!' she shouted, running along the fence towards a gate. I followed. 'He left the school grounds! He's on the other side of the fence!' she shouted. The policeman got out of the car and ran after us.

Maya threw the gate open and we both raced through it, then back along the fence to the two poles. I could still smell Geoffrey there. I put my nose to the ground. The smell was not as strong, but I could follow it. He had gone this way!

Then the smell faded, not two steps away from the fence. I stopped, lifting my nose into the wet air.

'What is it?' asked the policeman.

'He might have got into a car,' said Maya, worried. The policeman groaned.

I put my nose to the ground and backed up a few feet, and that's when I picked Geoffrey's scent up again. The trail was going the other way.

Maya gasped. 'She's got it. She's got him!'

I ran down the pavement, Maya and the policeman behind me. Beside us, water rushed down the gutter and gurgled down a storm drain. I leaped into the street and shoved my nose into the gap where the water was rushing from the street into the drain. The flowing water carried all sorts of smells with it – grass, dirt, rubbish, dead leaves, the faint scent of water itself – but I ignored those, concentrating every thought on my nose. If I needed to, I could have wiggled into that drain to follow the trail. But it turned out I didn't need to. I could smell Geoffrey strongly now. He was right in front of me, although I couldn't see him in the darkness. It was a good place for Geoffrey to hide, but I'd done it. I'd Found him!

I looked up at Maya.

'He's in there! He's in the sewer!' Maya shouted.

The policeman pulled a torch off his belt and knelt

down beside me in the rushing water to shine the light into the drain. We all saw it at the same time: the pale face of a frightened little boy.

'Geoffrey! It's OK; we're going to get you out of there!' Maya yelled to him. She knelt in the street, getting her uniform soaking wet as she strained to stretch her arm into the hole far enough to touch him.

But the water that was pouring into the drain had pushed Geoffrey back. He was clinging to the far wall of the sewer, to the edge of a black tunnel that stretched out behind him. The water roared around him, pouring past his body and into the long, dark space, and Maya could not reach him.

The sense of terror that was rising off Geoffrey was so strong it was blinding. I whined anxiously. My Finding of Geoffrey wasn't finished. He was there, so close to me, but I couldn't get to him, and neither could Maya. I understood that this Find would not truly be done until Geoffrey was out of the water.

Water. I'd never really liked it, and here was proof that I had been right. It might be fun to splash in the ocean where the water only reached my paws, or to jump into Maya's bath, but this water – I knew it was dangerous. It was deadly. It was going to hurt Geoffrey if we didn't finish Finding him soon.

'How did he get in there?' the policeman shouted.

'It's a tight fit; he must have squeezed in before it

was raining. It's really coming down!' Maya's voice was full of frustration.

A round circle made out of iron was set in the concrete right above Geoffrey's head. The policeman pulled at it with his fingers, trying to prise it open. He couldn't. 'I need to get a tyre iron!' he bellowed, and handed the torch to Maya before he ran off, his feet sloshing in the water.

I stayed crouched down by the opening to the drain, right beside Maya. Inside, I could see that Geoffrey was soaking wet and shivering with cold. His jacket was a thin yellow cagoule, with a hood pulled up over his head, but it wasn't doing much good.

'Hold on, OK, Geoffrey?' Maya repeated, leaning down so that Geoffrey could see her face. 'You hang on. We're going to get you out of there, OK?'

Geoffrey didn't answer. His eyes, in the yellow glow from Maya's torch, were dull, as if he hadn't heard her or he didn't care.

I heard a siren wailing, and in less than a minute a police car swung around the corner and braked right beside us, skidding a little on the wet street. The policeman jumped out and ran around to the back of the car.

'Fire and Rescue are on the way!' he shouted.

'There's no time!' Maya shouted back. 'He's slipping into the water!'

Maya was very afraid. I yawned with my own fear,

panting with it. We had to get Geoffrey out of the water!

The policeman grabbed something from the trunk and ran back to us with a long, thin rod of iron in one hand. 'Geoffrey, hang on! Don't let go!' Maya yelled. The policeman slipped one end of the metal rod under the edge of the circular plate in the cement, and he leaned on it hard. When Maya jumped up to watch, I went with her.

The policeman grunted with effort. The plate tipped with a *crack* and then flipped up, falling over on to the pavement with a clang that hurt my ears. Where the plate had been there was now a hole that went straight down to the sewer.

Geoffrey looked up, startled by the clang of the iron plate falling and the light that streamed down over him. It was only dim, grey light, drenched by the rain, but it must have seemed bright to him.

A splatter of mud fell on to Geoffrey's cheek. He lifted one hand to wipe it away.

'Geoffrey! Hang on!' Maya called out.

But he only had one hand on the wall now, and one hand was not strong enough. The water pushed hard against him, and he looked up at us for one moment before he was swept away into the tunnel.

'Geoffrey!' Maya screamed.

I was still on Find, so I didn't hesitate for a moment. I didn't like the look of that black rushing water at all, but it was carrying the boy away. I knew I had to follow.

I was terrified. I thought of my dreams of the boy Ethan. He'd sunk down into the water. Then Jakob had done the same thing. They had both needed me to save them. Now Geoffrey needed that, too. Could I do it?

I plunged headfirst into the water and was swept along the tunnel after Geoffrey.

18

It was dark in the tunnel; I wasn't even sure which way to swim. My nose broke the surface, and I gasped in a breath, choking as black water surged into my mouth. The top of my head scraped against the tunnel and then the water pulled me down again, wrestling with me, rolling me over and over.

I'd wrestled with Jakob and Al, with Maya, with my littermates long ago. That had been fun. This wasn't. I was being tumbled and dragged, not even sure where the water was going or how I could swim to shore.

And Geoffrey's scent was here, too, washed this way and that by the current. I would catch a hint of it and then it would disappear. But I knew he was ahead of me, soundlessly fighting for his life.

Suddenly the water pulled me downhill. When my head surfaced again, I was able to paddle. The tunnel we'd been pulled through had joined another, larger one. The current was flowing through this tunnel even more quickly, but since it was bigger, there was more air space above the water.

I swam as hard as I could towards the smell of Geoffrey. I couldn't see him, but my nose told me he was close, perhaps only a yard or two away.

Then the smell vanished. I knew he had gone under.

When Jakob had been under the water, I'd dived down to reach him. It had been the right thing to do. He'd praised me; he'd called me a good dog. I had to do the same thing for Geoffrey.

I took a breath and forced myself under the surface of the water, paddling hard. That time before, I'd been able to see Jakob beneath me. Now I could see nothing as Geoffrey and I were both swept along. But I knew he was there, tumbling just beneath me. I strained, my mouth open, blind, and then I reached him. I had the hood of Geoffrey's cagoule in my mouth!

I heaved with my back legs and dug with my front paws. Together Geoffrey and I burst through the surface of the water.

I heard him coughing and choking as I kept his hood between my teeth. I was gagging myself, trying to get rid of the water in my throat without opening my jaws.

Whatever happened, I would not left Geoffrey go.

I could not swim in any direction except the one the water was already going. All my paddling feet could do was keep both of us up so that we could breathe. At first Geoffrey tried to help as well, by kicking his feet. But as we raced along the black tunnel, he slowly stopped. His body sagged down into the water, pulling down on the hood. I struggled to keep us both from sinking, but it was harder and harder. My jaw and neck were aching; my legs were slowing.

How was I going to save Geoffrey? I'd Found him, but that wasn't enough. The water was going to drag both of us under, unless I could get him somewhere safe.

But where was safe? There was only the rushing water and the hard concrete of the tunnel's surface.

Some weak light from far ahead flickered over the tunnel's walls and the water's surface. Light – that was good. Light might mean sunlight; it might mean Maya; it might mean people who would help us.

The light grew stronger, and a sound grew louder along with it. It was a deep, humming roar, and the walls of the tunnel echoed it back at us until it filled my ears. I tightened my grip on Geoffrey's hood. Something was about to happen. But what?

The light grew brighter and brighter all around us, and suddenly we burst out into daylight, tumbling down a cement chute and landing with a splash in a swiftly flowing river.

The force of the splash forced us both under, but luckily my back legs touched something firm beneath me – a rock, perhaps – and I shoved us up.

Geoffrey couldn't help me at all. He was limp, his head rolling from side to side as the waves pushed us. Water splashed over my head and into my nose. I forced my legs to move faster. We were out in the light now. There had to be somewhere safe that I could go.

The banks of the river had been lined with cement, so that the current pulled us between two slanting walls. I tugged Geoffrey towards one bank, but the current fought with me, trying to pull us both back into the centre of the river. The ache in my neck and jaw was getting worse. What if I lost my grip?

Then flashes of light caught my eye. Downstream, men with raincoats and torches were running towards the bank of the river.

But they were too slow, weren't they? And the river was too fast. Geoffrey and I would be pulled past them before they could get to us.

I heaved against the greedy water. It was trying to suck us down, to claim Geoffrey, but he was mine. I had Found him. I wasn't going to give him up!

Slowly, I began to inch us both closer to the bank where the men were running.

Two of the men plunged into the water. They were tied together with a rope, and the rope ran back to the other men waiting on the bank. The two in the water waded out, hip deep, straining their hands to catch us.

But we were not close enough. The water would sweep us past them.

No. No, I wouldn't let it! I dug in with my claws, as if the water were dirt and I could dig it out of my way. I paddled and heaved and put everything I had into aiming for the men's arms.

'Gotcha!' one of them shouted as Geoffrey and I slammed into them.

The people on the bank braced themselves as our weight pulled the rope taut. But no one fell. One of the men in the water grabbed my collar. The other man seized Geoffrey around his waist and hoisted him into the air.

I let Geoffrey's hood go. I knew he was safe now. I'd Found him and I'd taken him to people. I'd done my job.

The man kept holding my collar tight and throwing his weight against the pull of the quickly flowing water. The men on the bank pulled, too, and together the four of us thrashed our way to the shore.

I was last in the water. The man who held my collar was hoisted out, but he never let go of me. Lying on the concrete, he pulled and heaved at me, and I scrabbled at the steep bank with my tired, aching legs, and somehow I was out.

I flopped down on the marvellous solid ground and spat water out of my mouth. Several of the men were huddled around Geoffrey. I saw one squeeze his skinny chest, and a gush of brown water came out of his mouth. Then he was coughing and crying.

I heaved myself up with a cough and a sigh. It seemed my job was not quite over yet. People were supposed to be happy to be Found. Geoffrey was not happy. I limped over to him, without enough strength even to shake the water out of my drenched fur.

I lay down heavily next to Geoffrey, and he threw himself on to me, hugging my wet fur with all the strength he had left. I could feel him shaking. The fear was beginning to drain out of him, though, and my fear was going along with it.

Geoffrey was going to be OK. I had done my Work again. I was a good dog.

Geoffrey kept holding on to me as the men around us pulled off his cagoule and his shirt and his soggy jeans and wrapped blankets around him. 'You'll be OK, boy; you'll be OK,' one of them said. 'Is this your doggy? She saved your life.'

Geoffrey didn't answer, but he lifted his head to look into my eyes. I licked his cheek with one quick swipe of my tongue.

'Let's go!' someone shouted, and one of the men gently pulled Geoffrey's hands loose from my fur. They picked Geoffrey up and ran with him up a hill to a street. When they loaded him into a white truck, it took off with its siren screaming.

I stayed where I was. My legs were shaking with tiredness, and it was all I could do to lift my head enough to vomit out the river water that had got into me.

Then I put my head down on my paws and lay still, the cold rain pelting me.

The siren of a police car wailed, getting louder, coming closer. I glanced up the hill without lifting my head. 'Ellie!' Maya screamed. She slid and scrambled down the hill to my side. I was too tired to wag my tail, but I was glad to see her. If she wanted to play tug-of-war, though, that might have to wait until later.

Maya was soaking wet; tears and rainwater were mixing on her cheeks. She hugged me nearly as tightly as Geoffrey had done. 'You are a good dog, Ellie. You saved Geoffrey. You are such a good dog. I thought I'd lost you, Ellie.'

After a while, Maya stopped crying and helped me up the hill, holding my collar and talking to me gently. With her arms around my chest she hoisted me up into the back seat of the police car, and we drove straight to the place where the man in the white coat looked me over from my nose to my tail.

I spent the night there, which I wasn't too happy about. But in the morning I got to go back to Maya and Al's house. I was so stiff for the next few days that I could hardly move, but everything else was back to normal.

A few weeks later, Maya and I did School again. Only this time the big room was filled with grown-ups, not children. We sat up on a stage with lights in our eyes while a man talked in a loud voice. I wondered when Maya was going to talk and if the grown-ups would come and pet me as the children always did, but that didn't seem to be the plan this time.

After he was done talking, the man came over to me and put a second collar around my neck. I wondered why he was bothering to do this. I *had* my collar on already, and this other one was flimsy and silly. It hung too loosely and had a big, heavy metal dog tag on it that banged against my chest when I walked.

The man also pinned something on Maya's uniform, and everybody clapped. She knelt down beside me while even brighter lights flashed around us, like lightning with no thunder.

It wasn't as interesting as Work or as real School. But I felt Maya's pride and love as she whispered that I was a good dog.

Then Maya got back up. 'Ellie, Come. I have a surprise for you.'

She walked with me off the stage. All the people who had been watching us were now standing up, talking in groups. A lot of them stopped to talk to Maya or shake her hand and she smiled back happily, but she kept moving. I stayed by her side.

Then she stopped. 'There, Ellie. See?'

I looked through legs, most of them in dark blue trousers, and I saw why Maya had brought me here.

A man was standing by himself, wearing a suit and tie, with a small smile on his face. The man was Jakob.

Maya let go of my leash and I bounded over to him. He stooped down, scratching my ears. 'How are you, Ellie! Look how grey you're getting.' He turned to a woman standing a little way behind him, with a girl in her arms. The girl looked to be a year or two younger than Geoffrey, and her grin was far wider than Jakob's.

'Daddy used to work with Ellie,' the woman holding her said. 'Did you know that, Alyssa?'

'Yes,' the girl said, squirming to get down. 'I want to stroke Ellie!'

'Can she, Jakob?' the woman asked.

'Of course.'

Alyssa ran forward and hugged me. I braced myself so she would not tip me over, and I licked her face. She giggled, and Jakob laughed.

I had never heard Jakob laugh like that before.

Over Alyssa's head, I looked at Jakob. He was so

different from when I'd lived and Worked with him. The coldness inside had gone away.

'I'm glad you're doing this community outreach programme,' Jakob told Maya. 'A dog like Ellie needs to work.'

I heard the word 'work' and wagged my tail as Jakob came and knelt down beside Alyssa and me. But there was no urgency in the word, no sense that we were about to Find anyone. Jakob just always talked about work. That was his way.

Maya hovered in the background, exchanging smiles with the woman who'd been holding Alyssa. She was the girl's mother, I realized. And Jakob was the girl's father. He had a family now, and he was happy.

That's what was different. In all the time I had known him, Jakob had never been happy.

I had never thought that Jakob might be lost or might need saving. He was the one who helped me save other people. But now it almost felt as if Jakob had finally been Found.

'We've got to get you home, honey,' the woman said to the girl.

'Can Ellie come?' Alyssa asked.

Everybody laughed.

It was nice to be there with both Maya and Jakob. I eased down to the floor, so happy I thought I might take a nap.

'Ellie,' Jakob said. He bent down and took hold of my face gently, looking into my eyes.

The feel of his rough hands on my fur took me back to when I was a puppy, first learning my Work. I wagged my tail, thumping it on the floor. I knew that soon I'd go home with Maya, that my place and my Work was with her now. But I was still full of love for this man.

'Good girl,' Jakob said gently, and I heard tenderness in his voice. I could tell that he loved Alyssa and her mother, and for the first time I could sense that he also loved me.

'A good dog,' Jakob told me. 'Ellie, you're a good dog.'

More About
Search-and-Rescue Dogs

Ellie is a search-and-rescue dog. She's trained to find people who are lost. In real life, dogs like Ellie do this kind of work every day. Handlers like Jakob and Maya work hard to train their dogs – and themselves – to do what is needed to find people in trouble.

What kind of jobs do search-and-rescue dogs do?
Some search-and-rescue dogs find live people, and others look for dead bodies. Some are trained for wilderness work or water rescue. Others find people who have been trapped in a collapsed building or hurt in a disaster. Ellie is trained to search for living people.

What does a search-and-rescue dog need to do?
A search-and-rescue dog must learn to obey its handler's commands, to find the scent trails left by a person, and to let its handler know that it has found something

important. Some dogs bark to alert their handlers; others use body language, such as the angle of the ears or the tension of the body. The dog must also be able to climb, balance on wobbly surfaces, crawl through tunnels, and become comfortable riding in cars, trucks, aeroplanes, helicopters, and maybe even ski lifts or boats, depending on the kind of rescues it will be doing.

What kind of dog can be a search-and-rescue dog?
It doesn't take a particular breed to become a search-and-rescue dog. Almost any breed, or a mixed-breed dog, can do the job, as long as it is strong enough. Bloodhounds are particularly good at following scent trails. St Bernards are experts at working in snow; their thick coats keep them warm and their strong legs and big feet help them clamber through drifts. Newfoundlands are good swimmers and have strong instincts for water rescue. (Sometimes they even try to 'save' swimmers who don't want to be saved!) Labrador retrievers, Belgian Malinois, Border collies, golden retrievers, and German shepherds (like Ellie) are also common search-and-rescue dogs.

When trainers are looking for a puppy that might grow up to be a good search-and-rescue dog, one of the first things they look for is how the puppy plays. Playing is a puppy's work. A young dog who will play with a ball or a toy for a long time, without getting tired or distracted or wandering off to do something else, might make a good search-and-rescue dog. A puppy who is focused on play may grow up to be a dog who is focused on work, who will not give up until the job is done.

When Jakob plays with Ellie and the other puppies in her litter, he is actually checking to see which of them might grow up to be a good rescue dog. Ellie shows Jakob that she is smart, focused, and willing to follow his commands, which is why he chooses her.

How is a dog trained to do search-and-rescue work?

Training, at first, is a game that the dog plays. A dog who loves playing will come to think of its training simply as another game. A dog might first learn to find its owner. The owner runs away, usually with the dog's favourite toy, so that the dog can see her leave. Then the dog is allowed to chase her. Once the dog finds the owner, the owner plays and wrestles with her, letting the dog see how excited and pleased she is. The entire purpose of this early training is to make the dog think that finding people is marvellous fun!

Once the dog is good at finding its owner, it will move on to finding different people. The people hide in more and more difficult places, seeing whether the dog can locate them. Each time the dog finds someone, that person acts delighted to be found, and makes sure to play with the dog as a reward. This is the kind of training that Ellie is actually doing when she thinks she is playing Find Wally.

A dog must also practise climbing and balancing, so that it will be confident walking on any kind of surface. Some dogs (like Ellie) learn to be put in a special harness and lifted by a rope, so that they can be lowered down or pulled up cliffs, holes, shafts, or even carried by helicopters. Dogs who will do water rescue must learn to swim four miles or more in the open ocean.

Training a search-and-rescue dog takes up to two years. A dog (and its handler) will continue to train and practise as long as it is working.

What kind of training does the dog's handler have to do?

A lot! Besides learning to work with a dog, handlers have to master skills like first aid (for people and dogs), map reading, using a compass, how to survive in the wilderness, how to preserve a crime scene, and more. They also must be in good physical shape (as Maya learns) so that they can keep up with a running dog and track people through miles of wilderness if they need to.

Who can be a search-and-rescue dog handler?

Police officers and firefighters may get special training to work with search-and-rescue dogs. Some people also volunteer to train their own dogs and help in search efforts. These people may work other jobs most of the time, but bring their dogs to help if someone is lost, or if there is a disaster and many people need help.

How do search-and-rescue dogs find people?

With their noses! A dog's nose is about a million times as sensitive as a human's. Dogs may follow scents on the air or on the ground. In either case, they are smelling the same thing: tiny pieces of hair and skin too small to be seen. People shed bits of their hair and skin all day long without knowing it. Dogs can smell these traces and follow them to the person they are hunting for.

It's easiest for a dog to follow a trail on a damp day without much wind, when the ground is a little bit warmer than the air. Those bits of hair and skin will cling to the ground for a long time on a day like that. Luckily for Geoffrey, it's that kind of day when he climbs into the sewer and gets trapped there. That means it's easier for Ellie to pick up his scent (even with her injured nose) than it would have been on a hot, dry day – as long as she can find him before the rain washes all his skin and hair away.

A DOG'S PURPOSE

Bailey's Story

W. Bruce Cameron

When Bailey meets eight-year-old Ethan, he
quickly figures out his purpose: to play with the
boy, to explore the farm during summers with
the boy and to tidy the boy's dishes by licking
them clean (only when Mum isn't watching).
But Bailey soon learns that life isn't always
so simple, and that there can be no greater
purpose than to protect the boy he loves.